The Panel.

Table of Contents

A work of fiction by Andy Gilbert

Preface & Warning

I have the utmost respect for the Police and the work they do under the most trying circumstances throughout NZ and I really should emphasise that any similarity to any person living or dead, in this novel, is a sheer coincidence.

Further I should add that I have based this story in Rotorua as it is a town I know well. The story could be based in any town or city around New Zealand and I would go to great lengths to emphasize that comment.

Copying and using

THE WRITER SPECIFICALLY cancels any reproduction in part or in whole of this work. Any such permission needs to have been given in writing by the Author and at all times the copyright of this work is retained by the Author.

Chapter 1

Monday

So, it's my turn to walk over and get the coffee. Out the back door and over to the library café. The library doesn't open until 9.00, but at the Café, they're open at 7.30 to get the early punters and they do make a decent cup of coffee. Annie is the girl that usually covers the early shift and I get on quite well with her. She's quite nice looking but probably a bit young for me. She'd be mid-thirties and I'm mid-forties although I reckon one or two of the younger PC's have taken a shine to her.

Annie has the order ready, three flat whites with one sugar, two sugars and three sugars and a long black for the sergeant. Annie mentions that one of the new plods is a week behind with their payment, so I make a note to mention it to him.

Strolling back over to the back door of the temporary Police station on Fenton St and there's some prat having a kip in the back of the rubbish skip. Not really my problem so I give a tap on the back door which is opened by the Sarge.

"Hey, Sarge, there's some idiot asleep in the skip. Can you get one of your PCs to give him a nudge and then tell him to bugger off?"

The Sarge ducks back inside and says something to one of the new PC's and then stands aside for me to deliver the coffee.

One long black for the Sarge, a flat white for me with one sugar and the two flat whites for the two PC's. As I was sharing the coffee, I could vaguely hear the Sergeant's voice behind me. I think it was the tone of his voice that got my attention.

"Oh bloody hell, lad. Is that the first dead body you've seen?' followed quickly by "Oh no! if you've puked on my shoes there'll be hell to pay. No! stay outside and put up the SOCO tape. That's an active crime scene you've just thrown up on. Stay there and I'll get the DS to come and have a look."

Then I heard him say, "Here!" Then there was a pause. "The Scene of Crime tape. Well go and get it then!"

Then he turned round to look at me. "Mark. You might want to have a look at this. Turns out the prat wasn't having a kip, and that bloody PC has puked all over your crime scene!"

" Oh well", I thought to myself. "Maybe today does have something going for it!"

I take a slow sip of my coffee and stroll outside, still holding onto my cup.

The PC looks a bit green around the gills and he's busy putting up the SOCO tape as he has been told to. I'm having a look at the PC and it's fairly obvious our newest PC has no desire to look at the body in the rubbish skip.

I'm always the helpful type and I couldn't resist having a dig at the new PC. "Get used to it, Constable! It doesn't get any better, but the more of them you see, the easier it becomes."

Without a word, he continued with taping the scene while I had a look at the victim.

Young, probably mid-twenties. Possibly, no make that 'probably' Māori. Age around 25 to 30. He sort of looked familiar but I couldn't immediately place him. Well, I couldn't really get a good look at his face. His head was towards the middle of the skip and his feet were just about touching the lower end. Weight probably around 150 to 180 pounds so whoever shoved him in had to be fairly strong. Why did I think he was put in there postmortem? I had a look at the ground around the front of the skip and there were definite drag marks from around two or three feet away. Yep. Definitely tossed in the skip after dying. No obvious wounds or bullet holes etc, so how did he die? I couldn't see any traces of blood on the body so did he fall in and fall asleep, or what? There were no fresh tyre marks leading to or going away from the skip. The rubbish skip size was one of those ten cubic meter jobs. About five feet high at the front and about three foot high at the open end. Obviously, they'd have tossed him into the skip from the lower end. Beyond that, there wasn't that much to glean from the scene.

Although it wasn't that bad, the new PC puking on the crime scene didn't make life any easier for me. Most of the evidence was in or around the Rubbish Skip and the new PC had actually turned away before he puked so there was no real damage done to the crime scene.

By this time, the few members of the squad who were still housed in the former 'temporary' Police Station were wandering out to see what the fuss was all about. Also, there were a few from the new Police Station on the opposite side of Fenton St who had arrived on the scene. I asked the PC to keep everybody back from my possible crime scene. More than a few were loudly asking who had thrown up around the skip. The PC was keeping his mouth shut until the Sarge pointed out the offender. Although it wasn't my role to stop the merriment, I did shoot an enquiring glance at those who had reacted the same way to their first dead body. That seemed to shut most of the rest of them up. If the DS was taking it seriously, then maybe the rest of them should also be taking it seriously. Low and behold, around the corner walked the new acting Chief inspector, Eru Mahana. That's just what I needed. The Acting CI and I had something of a history which didn't make for an easy relationship.

The photographer also arrived, and I busied myself telling him what shots I wanted.

Then, lo and behold. Mike Myles, the pathology guy arrived.

"Greetings Mark. I heard on the scanner about the body and thought I'd stop on my way to work. Is this one for me?"

"I'd say so, Mike. No obvious sign of a stab or bullet wound so maybe you can give us a clue. Indications are he was killed and tossed into the skip. There are drag marks for a few feet, See here."

As I was pointing out the drag marks Mike was starting to get excited.

"No fresh tyre marks either way. So did he walk here or was he coerced?" Mike, bless him, loved any hint of a mystery.

"Discovered this morning, by me at around 7.45 am. After that, it's down to what you can come up with."

"I'll make it a priority one!"

I had a sudden brainwave. Surely the cop shop would have a CCTV of the whole thing. As I turned around to see where the camera would be, I was confused because I couldn't see any camera. The Sarge had rejoined me at the back door to the station. "Watch out, Mark, his highness is coming round the corner." Then he realised the ACI was already on site! "Oh good morning, Sir. Could I ask you to step away from the DS's crime scene? Protocol until we get it examined."

The Acting CI muttered something under his breath but did step back a couple of paces.

"Sarge, whatever happened to the cameras that were on this area?"

"Gone! With the budget blowout on the new building, our friend over there (the acting CI) reckoned we needed this one on the back gate of the new building. It went about a month ago."

Meanwhile, the Acting CI was staring at the PC who was guarding the crime scene. He motioned to the Sergeant. The Sarge mimed someone puking and the Acting CI turned on his heels and walked away to his nice shiny new office. By now the rest of the audience were turning around to return to their offices.

"That went well, Sarge," I said.

"Stuff it. He'll usually find something to moan about. At least now he's got the new PC puking on the job. That'll give him something to mess about with," said the Sarge.

Before I go much further, I suppose I'd better give you a rundown on the Staff at the Copshop.

At the top of the tree, locally, the big Boss is Acting Chief inspector Eru Mahana. He's sitting in his shiny new office in the New Copshop over the road on Fenton St. There's a little bit of history with the Acting CI and myself. He started in the next intake after me and for a while he was my beat partner while I walked the streets in the CBD. The history I mentioned related to him getting a bit of wacky baccy off a supplier while I had been roped into helping the CIB out with a stakeout. I mentioned it to him rather than seeing a promising young PC being booted out of force. Occasionally it suits me to remind him. When he worked with me, he was called Eddie. When he started rising through the ranks, he reverted to his Māori name of Eru. It sort of teed me off but to each their own.

For myself I'd grown up in the streets of South Manchester and gone into the force at the age of 19. Based out of Salford Nick, I'd gone through my training and probationary period without incident. I'd married a young girl straight out of Police College, and we'd set up house in Sale. Within six months we both knew we were not the right set up, so we split up and started the divorce meetings. In the meantime, a fellow PC I'd met in Salford had applied to join the force in New Zealand and settled in Rotorua. He was all enthusiastic about the place, so I came up with the idea that I'd come over and give it a go. A nice easy divorce later and her taking on the HP for the furniture and I'm on my way to Wellington to do the new police recruit stage all over again. The other PC was of course the Sarge and I'll go to a bit more detail later, on him. Right, after three months in Trentham I'm sent up to Rotorua, by good fortune. And I've been here ever since, other than three years in Napier.

The Sarge and I are basically straight talkers which will only get us so far on the promotion ladder so, after twenty years we have both made it to the rank of Sergeant and we are unlikely to get any further because neither of us speak the PC language that is expected if you want to go higher in life. The Sarge is called Dave Smith and to those who know him well, he's known as 'Ticker' Smith because he likes his shifts to run like a well-oiled machine. Dave started in the Salford Precinct a couple of years before I started. He and I were often on patrol together as we were like minded. He came out to New Zealand when they were struggling to get new recruits in New Zealand and it's probably Dave who got me into thinking about leaving England's pleasant shores for the new life in New Zealand. I arrived in New Zealand in 2000. And once I did the recruit training I was sent to Rotorua. Dave put me right to a few things and I have been here most of the time, since. Dave married a really nice Māori girl called Huia and they have a couple of kids. I've been invited a fair few times, over the years, to dinner at their place and, aside from the odd girl that Huia reckons I'd be good with, I've settled down onto New Zealand life well. Dave would be around 49 years old, so that would make me around 46.

Dave's job was to attend the CIB desk and be there when all the Detectives were out busy. One of his other jobs was to pick up anything that needed CIB input from when the Squad cars had to attend any situation during the night. With his twenty odd years of experience he was the perfect bloke to look after the CIB desk. He had a good eye and a good memory for names and faces. It was hard to put one across the Sarge, and he also kept us all on our toes when he thought we were getting a bit slack.

In the "spare rooms across the road at Fenton St" is the entire CIB branch which comprises of me as a Detective Sergeant. The Boss is Detective Inspector, Colin Woods, and the other two are Detective Constables, David Powell and Tim Cross. At the moment Colin, David and Tim are based at Hamilton Central Nick. It seems they have been having a spate of ram raids up in Hamilton and the locals are getting pissed off with their local nick getting no results. Off licenses and Dairy's seem to have been hit the most regularly. They have gathered every spare officer and sited them at locations around the city. The theory is that if they get a call about a ram raid they can have someone on site within a minute or two. It's working well and they have a dozen or more arrests under their belt. They will probably be there for at least another week so that leaves me to hold the fort at Rotorua. Fortunately, it's been fairly quiet here. With the increasing number of homeless being put up in motels around the town, Rotorua is seen as an easy mark for drifters and the like. I'd hate to work in the benefits office but here at the CIB we mostly have to put up with the drug use and the client base being somewhat centrally located for the drug dealers. To be honest, I've not had a whole lot to do over the last two or three weeks. So, this homicide/suicide is a bit of a welcome relief. It will at least give me something to do.

And, last but by no means least we have a couple of new plods working with us. When they graduate out of Trentham Police Academy, they get sent to a fairly big station such as Rotorua. the new plods get a couple of weeks with the Transport Dept (that was), then they have a couple of weeks with the CIB and then they get pushed out on patrol. This week I have the pleasure of keeping the two new plods occupied while they get the 'CIB experience'. They're pretty good lads but it is something of a tradition to give the new lads a hard time, and who am I to break a long tradition.

The two new plods are Dave Besant and Derek Allan. Just so you are up to speed, Dave is the new PC who chucked up over the corpse sitting in the rubbish skip out the back of our office!

That covers most of the staff that work over in the old 'temporary building' on Fenton St. For the most part we don't have too much to do with the shiny new office over the road. I reckon that when the Acting Chief Inspector asked for volunteers to work from the temporary building, Colin Woods jumped at the chance to stay in the old offices and be out of the new 'Acting Chief Inspectors' gaze so he could actually get some work done instead of us constantly looking over our shoulders and wondering what the new ACI was doing. Whatever, we've been here for a couple of years now and it doesn't look like we'll be moving any time soon.

It's a funny thing but most coppers I have known have a soft spot for certain crimes. For me, it's sexual assault or rape. It gets me wound up when I'm on that kind of case. For the Boss it's anything to do with robberies. Even something as simple as shoplifting he gets excited about. For the two DCs they are both hot on physical assaults. Maybe it's because they are quite well muscled but it's a thing all coppers have.

Oh yeah. I'd better put you right on how to talk to people. It's an understood thing that if you outrank someone you can call them by their first name or surname. If you are of equal rank, such as the Sarge and I, you usually use their rank unless it's a social occasion. If someone outranks you use their rank unless the senior ranked person says it's ok to call them by their first name and even then you have to be careful that it might just be for this occasion or a permanent social occasion such as the Boss and the Big Boss and their Rotary meetings. It can be quite tricky but, if in doubt, use their rank!

Oh, and I nearly forgot me. My name is Mark Hallam and I think I've told you everything else about me already. Let's move on!

Chapter 2

Right, getting back to the crime scene.

The new PC had put up the crime scene tape. The photographer was busy taking his pictures and the fingerprint guys had started their work. Unfortunately, there weren't many useful prints. The builders who had been working in our offices had pretty much smothered the refuse skip with their prints so that wasn't going to be any help in solving this case.

The Builders? There're probably half a dozen builders who are working on splitting up the offices from what used to be an all-in-one Police station, albeit temporarily. Now they are rigging it out for a new Law office to go right in opposite the new Police station. From what I have heard, the new Law office will be a bunch of those guys who have never partnered up with one of the bigger firms. I assume that if there are a dozen or more names on top of the door it will make them seem like a big firm. The builders are setting up the new offices and occasionally they use our office as a way of getting out to the rubbish skip. Until I gave all clear to the builders, they had to store all of their rubbish in the Law place they were fitting out.

At around 9.30 they took the victim away for an autopsy and I had a chance to look over the scene. Hopefully we might get an early notice on the autopsy from Mike Miles before 5.00pm. There wasn't too much to glean from the scene. Had the killer deliberately dumped the victim outside our back door? Probably too coincidental to think otherwise. Had he been working alone? Probably, as there wasn't any sign of a second set of footprints and the main set were all fairly smudged so we couldn't get any hints from there. About the only thing we could pick up from the set up was that the killer had walked the victim up to the rubbish skip and then killed him and then lifted the body up into the skip. So, the killer had to be a fairly strong bloke. Probably, given the strength needed, the killer wasn't a girl. Most of this was supposition worked out by me. I didn't have a fellow detective to work with, so it was pretty much down to me.

Oh, and one other thing, it turns out I did know the victim. It was a local bloke called Dave Tapsell. It seems he'd been up on a rape trial a few months before. Consent was the turning point in the trial. We knew the rape victim was the innocent party, but this guy had a brief that twisted the whole thing around and left sufficient doubt that the girl was deemed to have given consent. It's such a shame really, as the Boss had put in a lot of work on this case. Even the Police get a little bitter when such a travesty occurs but there was nothing, we could do about it. We just watched as the accused had walked past us and smiled. Then we found out that the Crown Prosecutor (CP) was dragging his feet on a retrial because of the lack of evidence, and it seemed as if the lad had got away with this one. It happens, but it doesn't make any of us happy!

After wandering the crime scene for a while I went back into the Sarge's cubicle and asked for someone to work with me. It's always better to have a backup when you're interviewing people. The Sarge offered me the new lad who had puked all over the crime scene, Dave Besant. The Sarge had a smile on his face when he suggested I take the new lad. It seemed that the new lad had to go and get changed out of his uniform because he'd puked on his trousers and as he would only need civvies if he was working me, then that seemed to cover all angles. Like I said, the Sarge was all for keeping things running like a well-oiled machine! And it was no use for me arguing with the Sarge. Once he set his mind to it, it was a done deal!

Instructing the new PC to go home and change into civvies and be back within a half hour, the Sarge and I had a chat about who our suspects could likely be.

The Sarge started with," Well, you've obviously got the family of the rape victim, then you have the Māori and the Mongrel mob. What about the Chinese? They'd have to be in the hunt for revenge?"

The Sarge was well versed with the local crime families. If that sounds well organised, it's a misnomer. The Chinese had a bit of the opium business going on. The Mongrel mob were known to have a bit of wacky baccy and meth going on and the Māori were also known for having an element of drug dealing among their perhaps 30% of the local populace.

The Sarge was going on with his chat about the probable villains in our town. Then he told the other new plod to bugger off home and come back in civvies.

"You might as well take both of the new guys with you give them an idea of how the CIB works and as a plus, it will take them out of my hair for the day."

That's just what I needed! And the Sarge was smiling when he gave me the good news!

One bonus of having the new Pc's to work with was that I also had to keep an eye out for any other business the CIB should be looking into. Having a couple of plods working with me, I could always send them out to a new investigation should the need arise. I'd leave my decision on the two plods until I had worked with them for a day or two.

It was now getting towards lunchtime and the two new plods were back in the temporary station. I called it lunchtime and told them we would go over to see the Chinese lads after lunch.

During lunchtime I was approached by one of the new Pc's to clarify the situation on where the various judges and magistrates handled the cases. I left this one over to the Sarge as it was one of his hot topics.

"Judges and magistrates and high court judges all deal with various levels of crimes. Even JP's can handle a crime if it is lower on the scale. What you have to remember is that all of the JP's and judges are real people. If they were on a promise last night and got their promise, they should be in a good mood."

I suggested he mention the traffic cop as this was a talk the Sarge had given before.

"Thank you Detective Sergeant, I was coming to that next. What if the Judge gets stopped by a traffic cop on his way in to court. Let's say he might have been a bit heavy footed coming down Fenton Street. He has a ticket for going at 62 k's an hour. How is that going to affect his mood for the day. Let's say he has a first case that involves a speeding citation, disputed, obviously. Is that going to make the judge more, or less impartial. Let's say it's the same officer that gave the judge his ticket that morning. More, or less impartial?

The two new PC's were in a quandary over this situation.

Then the Sarge shifted tack. "What if it was the Crown prosecutor? Or what about the defense lawyer?"

"What you lads have to remember is to make the most of a case when you give it to the Crown Prosecutor. You have to give him every chance to get a conviction. Even a jury can have one member or a couple of members having a bad day. Maybe it's something as stupid as not wanting to be on jury duty. You always have to remember that the all the judges and lawyers and even the bloody jurors are only your average joe blow. If you give it your best shot with the paperwork then you can only rely on the CP having a good day. If the guy gets off through a technicality, you put it down to bad luck. But you do try and not fall into that trap again! Always remember that everyone in the system is an ordinary bloke or bird. But it always helps if you get your paperwork as good as you can and give the next bloke up the line the best chance to do his job as good as he can. That's one of the reasons I am in with the CIB lads. Everything has to come across my desk. If I reckon your paperwork is up to speed it will usually get past the DI. Now sod off and leave the DS and I to have our lunch."

It was a speech the Sarge gave to every rookie, and it gave them something to think about.

After lunch, I walked the two plods around to Eruera St and walked past the upstairs access to where the Chinese gang usually met. As always with the Chinese I had rung to make an appointment first with them. It was something I knew they appreciated and it was no skin off my nose.

I asked the plods to take a note of what they saw when we walked past the Chinese hangout. Once we had walked past, we went and sat down outside 'Capers' and I asked them how they noticed about the place as we had walked past.

Dave said it was upstairs. So that was a lot of use. Derek said he thought it might be upstairs so it would be easier to defend against an attack. It looked like I was really going to have to go back to basics with these two.

I started to explain," Okay. Whenever you are going into a new territory you should always have an idea of who holds the best ground. Yes, it is upstairs so that might make it easier to defend against an attack. But you also have to look at the bigger picture. The stairs are barely wide enough for two people to go up them, so any attack has to be led by a single line of attackers. There is only one guy at the head of the stairs, and I can tell you that he has to give the ok before they open the door from the inside. He cannot open the door from the outside. There are probably a dozen guns inside the upstairs room, so they are well capable of withstanding an attack. Now, do you have any idea of how the Chinese deal with people who act against their people?"

Neither of the two new guys had any idea of what I was talking about. I really believe they only focus on teaching the law down at

Police College. This was Police 101 for dealing with the Chinese gangs. This was good stuff for any gangs of Chinese whether or not they were triads or whatever.

"Okay, now listen carefully. All the shopkeepers, the Chinese shopkeepers that is, pay a nominal fee to the Bosses upstairs. It's not much, somewhere between fifty and a couple of hundred but it's enough to get them committed to the Chinese way of doing things. We don't get hardly any complaints about shoplifters hitting the Chinese business owners and here's why. If the Chinese business owners catches a shoplifter in their place, they get on the phone to the blokes we are going to see, and they send a couple of blokes around to tidy up. For a first-time offender these blokes will bend back a finger until it breaks and then let them go. For a second offender, they will break two fingers. As far as I know there's never been a report of anyone chancing their arm for a third time! These guys are serious about protecting themselves. As I said before, there's probably a dozen or more guns up in the room. These are serious players, and they don't want us to sort out their dirty laundry. They also have fairly regular Mahjong games for high stakes and there is also a bit of opium smoked up there. If we leave them alone, they tend to look after their own problems, so we tend to leave them alone. Any questions. Oh and while I remember, Annie at the Library Café told me that one of you was a bit late in paying up for their coffees, this morning. That's the sort of thing that can give us a bad name. I don't care which one of you it is but get it tidied up, please."

"Okay, so if you have no further questions, let's go down and get the run around."

"Run around?"

"You'll see what I mean when we get there."

Strolling back down to the Mahjong place I asked them to keep their eyes open when we gained access. Actually, I probably said eyes and ears as well.

Walking up the stairs, I went first.

At the top step we were halted by the outside guard. In local terms, he was the receptionist, and he asked why we were there. When we asked to meet with Shi Low, he asked us to wait a minute.

I told the plods that we would have to wait while they moved the money into drawers and probably remove the opium.

It was within a minute and the door opened from the inside and we were granted access.

I walked into the room, and I couldn't see Shi Low, which was disappointing. A Chinese gentleman arose from the Mahjong table and approached us. So, I asked to speak with Shi Low.

He went back to the table and conversed with the one of the guys sat down, in Chinese. When the guy came back to me to translate their conversation, I held a hand up. "Please tell Shi Low I know he has a better Kiwi accent than I do, and also tell him I also know that this gentleman is not Shi Low. I would prefer to speak to Shi Low direct."

From the back room an older gentleman came forward. It was almost as if he was waiting for us to rumble the phony.

"Mr. Detective Sergeant. We were expecting a visit from you. Please, step into my office."

Obviously, the invitation was for me only, so I asked the two new guys to stay with the others while Shi Low stepped back and ushered me into his private office. Both of the new plods were a bit askance that we left them alone for the most part. But it has worked since the Chinese started coming in about 15 years ago.

I'd only met Shi Low once before and that was while I was in the presence of my Boss so, on that occasion, I'd been the one to stay in the room with the Mahjong players. I was surprised at how well-furnished Shi Low's office was. Red and Gold Silk tapestries were everywhere, and a few obviously expensive jade sculptures were dotted around the room.

Shi Low opened the conversation with, "May I offer you some tea, Detective Sergeant. I appreciate you prefer it with milk but, ah here it is."

A young Chinese guy walked into the room with the tea. Dismissing him with a casual wave of his hand, Shi Low proceeded to pour it himself. It's a face thing so I sat back and watched. When we were both settled with a cup of tea in exquisitely fine China cups, Shi Low continued the conversation.

"You are here to find out if the killing of the Quai loh had anything to do with us, I assume."

"That would be a reasonable assumption. The father of the rape victim was a Chinese national."

"Let us dispel that enquiry for you, Detective Sergeant. If the Chinese had anything to do with it, we would have waited for at least six months to go past. By then your victim would have been completely surprised and possibly believed he had gotten away with his crime. If we had anything to do with his demise, we would have only then taken him to one of our many facilities where he would have faced his accuser. As you know, we have ways of making a person feel the need to unburden themselves. Once he had confessed to the crime, the first thing we would have done is to cut off the offending part, and then the victim, if he showed remorse, may have been set free. If not, he would never have been found by your men. To place someone in a rubbish receptacle such as what happened is a crudity which we would hope you would never have ascribed to our people."

Listening to Shi Low describe what he would have done made me shudder inwardly, but I kept my cool and continued to drink my tea.

"Thank you for explaining what you would have done although obviously this is a hypothetical situation for you are a peaceful people. Would you have any idea of who may have committed this particular murder?"

"I hear many rumours, but I have no idea if or how this particular murder was planned or by whom. I give you my assurance that should I hear any whisper I will pass it on to your Sergeant. I can confidently give you an assurance that the victim or her parents would not have planned this activity."

I interrupted, "because they have already approached you?"

"Oh, Detective Sergeant, that is something I will neither confirm nor deny. Let me say, we did meet and convey our condolences to the girl and her parents."

There was a pause at the end of his conversation which told me my suspicions were correct.

"If there is nothing else to discuss, Detective Sergeant, I have a busy afternoon ahead of me.

"Thank you for your time and the excellent cup of tea. I may call again if I have further questions."

"And there will always be a cup of tea ready for you."

With that the young Chinese guy from earlier entered the office and I was shown out. On the way out I collected the two new plods, and we went downstairs and wandered back to the Station. While on the way back I questioned the two new guys.

"Well, did you see anything untoward while I was talking to Shi Low?"

Derek spoke first. "Nothing unusual. They were having their game of Mahjong, but I didn't see any gambling. The young guy came into the office with the tea and that was about it."

"Okay, and well done for not noticing anything, you right pair of berks. There was gambling going on in front of your noses and you never spotted it. A Mahjong table has a hidden drawer in front of every player and that is where they keep their cash! Did they also speak in English in front of you?"

Dave chipped in with, "Yeah, they did. I thought that was nice of them."

I couldn't help but add, "You're a right pair of plonkers. They were taking the piss out of you. They were talking in English with one hand and gambling with the other. Never mind, we'll get you a little bit wiser before we send you back on patrol. "

When we got back to the temporary station, we wised up the Sarge. The Sarge was also thinking that the Chinese were innocent. Innocent, because it was probably too soon to act for them. When Dave Besant asked why, the Sarge explained it to both.

"The Chinese have lived in their land for thousands of years, probably. They have a different concept of time. Six months is a flick of their fingers. They are around for a long period. If one of them is wronged, they will avenge it or one of their successors will. Right, Detective Sergeant. Who is your next visit to?"

"Well the autopsy should be just done by now, so we'll head off to the morgue and see what Mike has for us."

When we got to the morgue, Mike was a happy Chappy.

"I've conducted the autopsy. I'd estimate the time of death to be somewhere around 10 o'clock to midnight last night. The victim probably stopped playing rugby a year or two back. Good muscle tone which is commensurate with his age but some signs of relaxed muscle tone which would indicate a bit more drinking and less exercise. I've done a blood screen and sent it off and we should get that back tomorrow. However... what's the matter with him?"

Mike is used to working with bodies or corpses and we were having this discussion while looking over the naked body. During this time Dave Besant was attempting to keep his puking face from following through with his actions when he first discovered the stiff in the skip that morning. I'm probably being kind when I add that the overall smell of the morgue wasn't helping either of the two new guys from adjusting to their surroundings.

Mike continued, "If you can't handle a dead body, don't go throwing up in my morgue! Piss off outside! Now, DS, if you look at this bloke's neck you'll see why I didn't pick it up first thing. Have you ever heard of Krav Magar?"

Derek Powell put in that he thought it was the style that the Israeli Intelligence taught their officers.

"Well done, that man," said Mike. "They also teach it at the SAS and to the guys that work for Intelligence squads around the world. See, what our victim was subjected to is a neck snap, and it was done by a pro!"

Adjusting the body so we were able to look at the side of the neck, Mike continued, "See here. The neck was snapped, clean as a whistle and the guy was dead within a second or so. I've opened the side of the cervical region so we can take a look."

That's when Derek also decided he had seen enough, went green at the gills and shot out of the door.

"Just give me the details, Mike. I don't really need to see the broken bones, thanks." Even I was starting to feel just a little queasy looking at something that obviously fascinated Mike.

"OK, if you insist. There was no other reason for the victim to die other than the broken neck so, subject to the toxicity report, I'm putting it down as a broken neck and the victim as a homicide victim."

Mike was a little bit miffed. He'd obviously gone to a bit of a bother with his autopsy, and he felt a little let down that none of the boys from the Cop Shop were too interested in all of the gruesome details! By now we were in Mike's office and the plods had joined us again.

Mike laid the body back on the slab while our two fearless plods returned to the scene. Mike took us into his office there. He explained how Krav Magar went about their somewhat gruesome business.

'Okay. Here's how the Karav Magar guys teach it.'

He demonstrated on Derek despite his protestations.

"Push the head sharply to one side, doesn't matter which way it goes, and then put the other hand interlocked with the first elbow or just gripping it if you can't get it right in, and yank hard in the opposite direction the neck is turned. It's really simple and over in a couple of seconds. I believe they used to use this to overpower sentries and the like or just as a killing tool when you weren't armed."

Derek flexed his head when the pressure was eased.

Mike continued," I believe they teach it now at most advanced killing schools. So, your killer is likely to be ex SAS or something similar, more than likely ex-military."

Mike was standing there as if he expected some applause for his deductive reasoning and how he had worked it out. I did oblige and then we wrapped up the chat with Mike and went back to the station and filled the Sarge in. The Sarge was impressed with Mike's reasoning and reaffirmed that Mike loved anything with a bit of mystery to it.

That brought us neatly to a little after five, so we headed home for the day. Not before the Sarge reminded the two new plods to wear civvies as they would be tailing me around for a few days.

Thanks Sarge!

I went home to my little bachelor pad. I had a three-bed unit on Holland St. Bought it before the prices went crazy as a reward to myself for passing the Sergeant's exam.

Once I'd had my tea, I went up to the rape victim's home. I had to interview them to eliminate them from our enquiries, but I already knew from the visit to the Chinese today that I would get no help from the rape victim. Any form of retribution would have been left to Shi Low and he would probably have waited at least six months before he acted. It was the way the Chinese worked.

I'd gotten to know the family fairly well during their ordeal, so I was warmly welcomed when I went to their home in Sunset Heights.

"Good evening, Detective Sergeant. We were expecting you to visit."

"Good evening, Chen. I take it your daughter is home?"

I was ushered into the lounge and given a cup of tea as I sat down." Good evening, Marie. You will no doubt have heard of the murder today."

The father spoke for all of them. "Yes, and we have already had a phone call from Shi Low to suggest we should expect you over the next few days."

"Well that makes my job a little easier. Obviously, I have to eliminate you from our enquiries, so where were you all at between 10 and midnight last night."

Obviously, they all had an alibi, which was what I had expected. This family were not the type to seek out revenge, when they already had intimated the issue with Shi Low. I still felt quite sorry for Marie, the victim of the rape. She'd quite gone into her shell since the trial, and it was not nice to see a bright and bubbly girl so obviously withdrawn.

After a few further pleasantries with the family, I left them and went home.

I did have a look at the Krav Magar items on You tube before I went to sleep. I picked up a few hints from the Krav Magar site that might be useful. Especially if ever, someone tried the neck break maneuver on me. It involved you getting an arm up inside of the second arm so the strength of the humerus was your main defence. I went to bed around 11.00 and slept quite well.

Tuesday

I was in at my usual time of around 7.30am and still did not beat the Sarge into the office. I walked over for the coffees and was pleased to hear that whichever one of the new plods was guilty, they had at least gone over and settled their account with Annie.

Annie was her usual talkative self when I got over there. It seems that the whole town knew about the murder and there were several suggestions as to who the victim could be. When I told her who it was, she let out a gasp of surprise. "Isn't he the one you had for the rape trial and the prick got off?"

Yeah, she was right on the button, and she also mentioned that he occasionally came in for a coffee on his way to work. He worked at the Council depot on the Eastside and was quite the charmer when he wanted to be. By that I figured he had tried to get his charms to work on Annie but she had easily resisted his advances.

Collecting my four coffees I walked over to the back door of the cop shop and handed them out. The two new plods were still in civvies when I handed out their coffees.

"Right you pair. Today we get down to real CIB work, which is bloody boring. Derek, I want you to tell me everything we know about the victim. Dave, I want you to get me anything over the last five years and especially any case where the victim might have had this neck break done on them. You've got a couple of hours and then we'll head out and see some more villains. Well, off you go then!"

I should point out here that our busiest days in the CIB were after the Friday and Saturday nights. After that, it was the Thursday and Sunday nights with hardly anything happening on the Monday, Tuesday and Wednesday nights.

I sat with the Sarge for a half an hour which was really to bring him up to date on my visit last night with the rape victim and their family. He had nothing for us to busy ourselves with from the Squaddies the previous night, so today was also a good way to let the two new guys see how boring CIB work could be. After an hour Derek was back with all of the info I needed, so I sent him back to assist the other guy, Dave, with his research.

I have to say that the two new plods were well clued up on computers. in NZ We used the NCIS programme which probably stands for the National Criminal Information systems. When I gave the task to the new lads they were talking in a foreign language. When I asked them to explain they started going on about 'Search parameters' and 'sort characteristics'. I left them to it once they had explained it and it had totally gone over my head.

After that I pretty much perused the papers, online, to keep myself updated on the larger picture. I was pleased to read that the Hamilton extended squad had a few successes with their ram raiders.

At around 9.30 am I got the two new plods together and gave them a rundown of the day's plans. In turn, they gave me what their research had dug up. As far as yesterday's victim was concerned there wasn't too much to pick over. A shop lifting spree when he was about fourteen, driving without a license when he was sixteen, and a DUI when he was twenty-one. The next time he came to our attention was when he allegedly raped the girl last year and his subsequent trial and acquittal.

Dave on the other hand had a bit more to tell. Dave actually liked doing the research and he had some quite good intel to deliver. There were probably four cases in the last five years that might have used the neck snap technique. Two of them were an open verdict where the coroner couldn't really decide the cause of death, and the other two were a mystery. One suggested a probable cause of death by misadventure. A cyclist going down an MTB trail which resulted in a broken neck and the other was also an open verdict with no cause of death being attributed. I filed their paperwork with a mental note to look at it later.

I had decided that we would visit the Mongrel Mob first. Once you get inside with them, they are nowhere near as bad as you would first think. I had a quite reasonable relationship with Ronnie who was the leader of the local Mob. Don't get me wrong, they were still drug dealers and peddlers of stolen goods, but, as Ronnie said, "no one's perfect!'

We got in my motor to drive up to View Road. Well, it's a side road off View Road. We parked outside the gang HQ, and I motioned the two plods to step out of the car and stand on the pavement.

"Okay, you two. This is the headquarters of the Mongrel Mob in Rotorua. Firstly, I reckon there is more firepower inside that building than there is back in the armed offenders' squad room back at the nick. The second thing you have to know is they have a code amongst themselves. Never disrespect the patch or you're in for a whole load of trouble. Thirdly, we are guests in their 'home' and should act accordingly, and fourthly, for god's sake do not make any sudden moves!"

With that I stepped boldly forward and knocked on the gate.

There was the sound of something being moved from across the doors inside and then we were let inside. I produced my warrant card and told the bloke who let us in that I would like to speak to Ronnie. So far so good and we were ushered inside and up the stairs.

We were shown into a room with maybe a half-dozen gang members present. Given that I had just had a word with the two new blokes, I made the first mistake. I wandered forward to shake hands with Ronnie, the leader, when a guy, I had never seen before, shoved a double barreled 12 bore into my chest.

I looked at Ronnie, who grinned, and at the new guy who had the gun in my chest. I confidently put my hand on the barrel and pushed it sideways and placed it on the chest of Derek. Looking the guy squarely in the eyes I said, "if you're going to shoot anyone, shoot him. He's been a right pain in the arse all day!"

Ronnie burst out laughing, which was the desired effect, and he said, "Shit, you're a cool bastard Sarge!" Then he got up and shook my offered hand. "You fellers want a cup of tea?"

With that the tension in the room eased and, more importantly, the gun was lowered.

Ronnie spoke first, "You fellers want to ask me about whether the boys had anything to do with the murder outside your back door?"

Grateful to accept the offered cup of tea, we sat down around the table.

"You know how it is, Ronnie. So can you all account for your movement between 10 and midnight on Sunday night?"

Ronnie replied with, "And you know how it is, Sarge. We can all alibi ourselves being with each other, any night of the week you want."

"Okay, Ronnie. Let me ask a question off the record. Did you or your lads have anything to do with what happened at our back door!"

"Nah, Bro, not our style and you know that. And if we're asking questions off of the record, which one of your blokes puked all over the body?"

Without trying to drop anyone in it, Derek and I both pointed to Dave while at the same time denying anything like that ever happened.

Dave looked embarrassed, as he bloody should do, but Ronnie just said, "Don't worry, bro, you get used to seeing a bit of blood and it does go away." While most in the room laughed it off there was one Mongrel guy who looked a little bit sheepish, and he also got a bit of a windup.

I did like Ronnie and the rest of his lads. Yes, they were a mean bunch when they were fighting but I never saw that side of them. We probably stayed the best part of another half hour before we left. Once I got out and back to the car, I apologised for the gun incident and acknowledged that I had moved too quickly. Dave had some comment that he didn't like having a bloody 12 bore pointed at him. I told him to relax and that it probably wasn't even loaded. It took him a few seconds to realise that it probably was loaded but by that time we were on the way back to Nick.

I'd had a phone call from Mike Myles, so I returned the call.

When I eventually got through the hospital's extensions list, I was put through to Mike.

After brief pleasantries Mike came out with," Just had the tox screen back and the guy showed signs of regular cannabis use and get this, he'd been roofied!"

I asked Mike to explain further.

Mike continued, "Roofied! Rhopynol! The technical name is Flunitrazepam. Someone had spiked his drink. You know, poured a Mickey Finn into his beer. The guy was pretty well out of it when he left the pub. He walked to his car and was pretty much out on his feet. If you get the video from the pub car park, you might have the killer!"

I thanked Mike for his efforts and turned around to Derek.

"Okay, we need to find out which pub our victim was drinking at and get the video footage from the car park and also any video from inside of the bar that might show who spiked the guy's drink. Just have a ring round the pubs and mention my name if you have any problems. Dave, you can take the other half of the list and do some ringing around. It shouldn't take too long. There're only twenty or fifty pubs in his town. Well. Get on with it then!"

I turned around and had an update with the Sarge. I always found it useful to speak to another person when I was on a case. They often reminded me about something within their own circle of events, that and the fact that the Sarge was a regular fountain of information about things in Rotorua.

"Okay, you two. We'll have our lunch and then we'll go and see the guys at the marae. We'll go to the victim's marae at Ohinemutu. That's probably where we'll get any proper information. Have either of you ever been to a Tangihanga?"

Neither of them had.

"Okay, so it will be a great experience for you. The ACI will be there as it is his own marae. You will need to be welcomed on so I might let the ACI explain that to you. "

I rang Mike, the Pathologist, "Mike, I might need a favour from you. It's up to you when you release the body. Can you hang on to it until you get my call."

Typically, Mike didn't ask questions of me. So that was good.

After lunch we headed out to Ohinemutu.

I'd been welcomed on to that marae when we first arrived in Rotorua, so I was fairly well clued up on the protocols. Or so I thought. The two new guys had not been welcomed on and I didn't really understand the protocols, so I told them to stay in the car.

I walked into the common ground in front of the marae and was greeted by a half dozen men. Most of them I had met a few times, but we still had to make the protocols, so I did the pressing of noses with them. I have to say, it felt good being warmly welcomed as such and I did feel a part of the marae family even though it was a solemn occasion. In a way I also felt a part of the loss of one of their tribal sons even though I did not hold him in particularly high regard. It's a strange way of talking about it, but I did feel one that I was one of the locals.

Mason spoke on behalf of the group. Mason was one of my favourite Māori blokes. He was a straight talker and you usually knew where you stood after he had spoken to you.

"Greetings, Detective Sergeant. "There followed a few pleasantries before we go down to the serious subjects.

Mason continued, "If it is alright with you, our group would like to hold a blessing of the site of the incident tomorrow morning. Would nine o'clock be convenient with your office?" I agreed and added that it would be a great honour to be included in that blessing. Obviously the ACI would be there as well. I made a mental note that I really needed to mention the Blessing to him. I should also mention to the builders that they couldn't put any of their rubbish in the bin for maybe an hour or so after the blessing. Maybe I was being a bit too sensitive with the protocols, but it pays to be extra cautious where the Elders are concerned.

Mason also mentioned that it was a source of inconvenience that the coroner was unwilling to release the body of the victim so he could be welcomed on to his home marae.

Taking my cue, I stepped back, with Mason's permission, and rang Mike. I asked him firmly to release the body of the victim and that there were protocols to be followed.

Mike, on the other end of the line, was saying that I only had to ask nicely, and it would be done. I repeated my request a little more firmly.

Mike was on the other end of the line when it clicked that I was putting on a show for Mason's benefit. "Whatever my master wants." He was trying to be funny, and it was not helping me keep a straight face.

We agreed that the body could be picked up immediately and the whole atmosphere on the marae eased.

Mason said thank you and then we got down to talking about the whole sad situation.

I can appreciate how sad it must be for a family to lose one of their members at an entirely unexpected stage of life. What I found hard to take on board was that the particular family member was without the dignity and mana of the group that I was talking to. I put it down to not talking ill of the dead. We confirmed the timing of the funeral or Tangihanga and I left the marae. It was not worth my while asking for people to alibi where they were on Sunday night. The entire Hapu was just too large to even contemplate that question.

Going back to the Nick I was fairly preoccupied with my thoughts and the two plods left me alone with my thoughts.

As I pulled up to the back of the temporary copshop I realised my motor was running a bit sluggishly.

I reminded myself to get it looked at and then went into the nick and reported the latest details to the Sarge.

I gave the two plods more instructions to see if anything further could be dug out from the few cases that Derek had come up with while I went on down to the service dealers that I had bought the car from.

I'd bought the car new as there was a deal going on with the local dealers that gave us a decent discount for purchasing through the Police.

I drove it straight into the service depot and the guy there said he'd have a look while I waited.

Now I know I'm fairly middle-aged but when I was first into cars, I tended to do the mechanics myself. Now it was all about plugging your laptop into the vehicles computer system and getting the laptop to do the hard work. Whatever!

The mechanic said I had a spark plug problem so while I was waiting for him to change that I wandered into the reception where I spotted Pete, the guy who sold me the car.

"Ello Sarge. I see you got that body out the back of your place. Any news?"

"Hi, Pete. Well we've got an ID. Turns out it was a lad who was up for rape a month or so back."

"Well, Well. From what I hear the prick finally got a bit of justice, then!"

I had to reply, "Yeah, but don't quote me on that!'

Before I had a chance at further conversation, the mechanic came through and told me It was all sorted. They'd replaced the number three spark plug and it should be right as rain, now.

It was about 5 minutes to 5'oclock so I went home and had an early night. I'm currently rewatching episodes of "Elementary" with Johnny Millar playing Sherlock Holmes. I cooked my tea and settled down for an evening watching the box.

If you ever do decide to go into the Police force and are looking for a nice eight to five job, don't think about the CIB. It was a rare treat when you got an undisturbed evening at home. That said, I'm not complaining about the job. More like telling it like it is!

Wednesday

As usual, I was in by 7.30 in the morning and wandered over to the coffee shop at the library, which somehow reminded me I had to ring the ACI to tell him about the blessing going on at the back of the temporary copshop at 9 am that morning.

Annie was her usual chatty self and she'd been able to tell her regulars about the identity of the victim, so she was quite happy. Going back over to the cop shop I reminded the Sarge and the two plods about the blessing and then I emailed the ACI. Within five minutes he was on the phone asking me about progress in the case and who was coming over from the marae and how many people we would be having present. Of course, there would have to be a special liaison officer for the local iwi so the ACI would sort that out. He might have been a bit disappointed with the lack of progress so far in the case, but he settled on ridiculing the new PC for throwing up at his first body. With that he instructed us all to be outside and available for the blessing. Fortunately, for us, the blessing party were going straight up to the morgue afterwards to escort the body down to the marae so we wouldn't be up for feeding them. Call it whatever you want, but I didn't appreciate the thoughts of a few outsiders crawling over my workspace, and I'm sure the Sarge also felt that way! By 9.00 there were maybe 8 members of the marae outside and the Police managed to muster 9 members. Well, it seemed important to the ACI!

Even though I did not understand a word of what they were saying the blessing was a nice and very pleasant exercise to be among. When the marae members left, they took along the ACI who was also a member of their marae and would help add dignity to the proceedings of escorting the body onto the marae.

That left the Sarge and me and the two plods to settle down and discuss what we had achieved so far.

We all agreed we had nothing! There was also nothing to report from the Sarge about anything the Squaddies had attended to the previous night.

I suppose the murder investigation had to be our main priority, with us being so undermanned. But we all agreed there was not one single shred of any evidence beyond the pathology report.

Derek had struck some success in that the victim had been drinking at the Palace tavern on Sunday night and the Palace tavern people were quite happy to give us any security footage they could come up with. At this time, I got a call from my real Boss. Detective Inspector Colin Woods, who was over in Hamilton.

He opened with, "G'day Mark, I hear you've got a body in the skip out the back of the office. Any progress?"

"Good to hear from you, Boss. Nothing to report at this point. I've been and seen the Chinese and the marae and the Mob. Nothing to report from there. Oh, and I've also been to see the rape victim's family. Nothing from there, either. It appears the Chinese might have been looking to do something about it but it's too early for them."

"Shi Low is fairly secretive, but I reckon if he says he had nothing to do with it, I'm inclined to believe him. Let me know if there's anything I can help you with, but the reason for ringing is, do you fancy coming over for a few beers on Friday and watching the Chiefs up against the Blues? Corporate box and free beers. Seems the Chief Inspector up here is pleased with what we have done, and he's got one of his mates to splash out on a few free tickets to the game. If you get too pissed, you can stay in my room. The Missus isn't coming until Saturday morning."

"Free beers and free tickets! That sounds a bit like me. You're on! Meet you at your hotel?"

"Be here by about 6.30 and we'll take it from there. See you then!"

My Boss wasn't the best at small talk, but still I'm on for a few beers and a game. That's got to be a plus.

Then we got back to the nitty gritty. I went up to the Palace Hotel and grabbed their tapes for Sunday evening. They only had tapes of the bar and for outside the pub entrance, but it might give us something to go on.

They were a little bit blurry, but it was the best lead so far. The victim had gone into the pub around 8.00pm and stayed there for most of the evening until around 10.15 then he'd gone outside looking a bit the worst for wear and walked towards the east. For those of you not familiar with Rotorua, he headed towards the Government Gardens.

He'd been with a few mates up until 9.30 and then the mates had gone and left him to drink alone until he left. We couldn't see which table he sat at other the fact he'd kept coming back to the bar to get his drink refreshed. While we watched, the Sarge kept chipping in with the names of those people he knew.

Charlie H.

Pete whatshisname, er Tapehana.

Dave Whatarau.

Mike Shorter.

Jerry Jelliman.

Peter, don't tell me, Peter Crawford.

Don't know him, or him, but that's Johnny Shirland.

It never ceased to amaze me how many people the Sarge had met in his time in Rotorua.

About all we could gain from the footage was that the victim had been in the pub and had been drinking with mates until the mates had left. There were a few people that the Sarge didn't know, but not that many.

Once we'd gone back to the beginning, the Sarge said," Hang on, no go back a bit. Well, I wouldn't have expected to see him in the Palace. That's Jeff, Jeff Whiteley. What the hell is he doing in the Palace?"

Jeff Whiteley was a local, well I suppose you'd call him a local VIP. Rotary member, Hospital board member local businessman.

"Is he worth a pull, Sarge?" asked Derek.

"Probably not, but it might be worth visiting him at his office."

With another lead not being that helpful we turned our attention to any other business we had on hand. One of the things was a suspicion that a local group of 'security men' were actually riding roughshod over the rights of the local homeless. There was also a suspicion that the 'security men' were actually dealing drugs!

I left the two plods doing some follow up work and I went back to View Rd to see the Mongrel Mob. Ronnie was up in his office (of sorts) and he invited me in. 'Yeah, I heard that some of those pricks are dealing. But they're nothing to do with us!"

This was more up my street. "So where are they getting supplies from?"

"From what I heard, they're getting it from Tauranga. But you didn't hear that from us fellers!" I liked Ronnie, he would often give us a few clues about what was going on in town. Provided it didn't interfere with his own business dealings.

Heading back to the nick I was mentally totting up how I would use the Info from Ronnie. I decided that it was probably best to ring the DI in Tauranga and see what I could find out.

Arriving back at the office I found that the ACI had grabbed my two plods and took them down to the Ohinemutu Marae to give them a few clues. I was quite happy with that, other than the fact that everything they would be taught would now be from a Māori perspective. For me it was important to have a more balanced point of view. I'll deal with that later, maybe!

I got on the phone to the DI in Tauranga. It turns out they had also been grabbed for the operation in Hamilton. I ended up speaking to the Detective Sergeant, which was good because I'd already met him once or twice.

Like Rotorua, Tauranga had been hammered when they wanted staff in Hamilton. Because Tauranga also had bases in Papamoa and the Western Bay they hadn't been hit quite as hard as us, but they were still down on numbers. Getting down to business I discovered that Tauranga was one of the biggest ports for drug import in the North Island. When they had a tip off about a big load coming in, the Tauranga boys were quite successful with interceptions, but the Sarge admitted there was too much coming in by smaller quantities. They had something of a hold on the traffic, as they knew how it was getting to Rotorua, but it was only when they were due for a big raid was there any interruption in supply. For our situation in Rotorua they were aware of the stuff being moved out and making it into Rotorua, but they couldn't help that much with the distribution in Rotorua.

For the afternoon I went and parked outside the Racecourse and watched the traffic flows. There were a few cars that went from one motel to the next, so I took a note of the license plates and decided I'd hand them off to the two plods. Well, it gave them something to do!

By five o'clock, I'd had enough so I went back to the nick to update the Sarge. The two new lads were there along with the ACI. I'd have thought I would have missed the ACI, but I was not that lucky.

The two plods were getting a 'remedial talk' by the ACI. It turns out the plods had to sit all day while the new people were welcomed on. It's quite a nice ceremony but it pales when you have to be a part of it ten times! And what was worse, since they had been welcomed early, they then had to sit with the Elders and be a part of the team welcoming newcomers on to the marae. They were both very familiar with the 'Hongi' which means the sharing of breath (I think) and it made them both a bit more aware of the strict protocols of entering the marae. They had had a local who had explained the protocols to them and who also kept with them and gave them the updates on who was who and where they ranked on the totem pole.

Eventually the ACI left, and the two new guys were allowed to go, which left just me and the Sarge.

"Well they've had a fair intro to the marae protocols, with the ACI making sure he was seen by everyone," I said.

The Sarge chuckled, "It gets worse! Young Dave there almost puked when he found it was an open coffin on display."

With that, I went home, and I cooked my tea. It's an old saying but when you get a crime, such as we'd had, they reckon you've 48 hours to solve it and after that the chances of it being an easy case go markedly downhill. Well, we'd had our 72 hours and we were still no closer to any solution.

Thursday

On Thursday I set the two plods up with a task.

"If the drugs are coming over from Tauranga, how are they coming over? What resources do we have at our disposal to research this question?"

I actually wanted them to use the Police database to do some research. To be fair, they did come up with several avenues to investigate. I was just a little bit impressed with them to be honest. For a couple of rookies, they did seem to come up with suggestions.

It was getting close to lunchtime when they got back to me, with their ideas.

They'd worked out a log of traffickers operating in and around the Tauranga area and seeing how often they came over to Rotorua. Then they checked if any patterns emerged with the local dealers. I thought that was pretty good of them! They had gone that extra bit and dug out traffic footage from out by the airport.

They did have a few regular trips between here and Tauranga, but they discovered that the local traders were mostly going the other way. So they were going the other way! They were actually going over to get their drug supplies from Tauranga.

At 11 o'clock I sent them up Arawa St with the task of finding out which businesses had any CCTV footage. I did know that the Belgian bar and the Subway had CCTV, but it wouldn't do any harm to find out if any other businesses had them and would they mind if we looked at their footage. I also figured the Court would probably have some CCTV footage, so I sent them there as well. They did well! They had probably a half dozen businesses over the block and they'd secured permission to view the footage.

In the afternoon I sent them out to sit outside the Racecourse and see if any of the previous day's patterns re-emerged. Overall, it was a successful day with any number of the previous days' visitors to the motels being flagged once again. And because they had done the digging there were several vehicles of interest to us. I rang them around 4pm to ask them to come in and tabulate their efforts.

It was actually a good idea of mine to give them all the scut work as they realised that the CIB was most definitely not the glamour and glitz that they show on TV and the bulk of it was basically scut work!

Chapter 3

F riday

On Friday morning I remembered to pack a case for going over to Hamilton for the game and I was still at work by 7.40 and wandered over to Annies's place to get the coffees. She was fairly busy with other customers, but she did ask me if I'd made any progress with the murder victim.

When I said no, I don't know if she believed me or whether she thought I was keeping things close to my chest. Whatever!

When I got back with the coffees there was a message from the ACI that he would be taking the two new guys to the Tangi at 9.00 am and they would probably be there most of the day. That quite suited me, as by inference, the ACI wasn't expecting me to be in attendance.

When I mentioned it to the guys, they were sufficiently polite to not show their displeasure. It might have helped that I agreed with the ACI and that it could be a good experience to go to a Tangi.

I had my coffee with Sarge and discussed what I was going to do with my day. He had a burglary for me to look at in Arawa St. I thought I'd put in an appearance at the burglary and then do the other business in Arawa St that had any footage on CCTV.

I waited until after 10.am and wandered up Arawa St. I attended the burglary first. It seemed like a professional job with gloves being worn etc. The owner reckoned he had already been done over a couple of times and he was unsure whether the Insurance companies would be up for cover for a third event. I said I'd get the fingerprint lads on the job but there was not a lot more I could do. Then I walked Arawa St looking for businesses that had security footage. By careful viewing and doing some backtracking I was able to work out that the victim had parked between the Subway and the Arawa bar. I had footage of the victim walking past the Subway but not going as far as the Arawa Bar. When I was wandering up and down the street, I came across a vehicle with probably four tickets on it. When I phoned the Sarge he was able to confirm that this was the victim's car! The Sarge arranged to get it towed and fingerprinted so I went back to the other businesses to check if the victim had got into another car. Sure enough, the victim was legless by the time he had left the bar and it appears some kind stranger had seen him and offered to drive him home.

Having examined the footage, I then went back to the station and reviewed the camera footage we had obtained from the Palace Hotel.

I was able to establish, eventually, that the kind stranger who had offered to drive the victim home had also been in the Hotel that night. Normally, I don't believe in coincidence, so Sarge and I went through the Palace Hotel footage again.

This time we were looking at the bloke in the footage. We were able to establish that the guy in the footage had made contact with the victim. It appeared that the guy had even bought the victim a beer. We couldn't really see when the roofie had been poured into the drink but we both noticed that the victim had been reasonably 'not drunk' before the event, but he was definitely showing signs of being the worse for a few beers after he had been bought a drink by our guy. When we watched the footage of the victim leaving the pub, he was definitely showing signs of having too much to drink. And we also noticed that the bloke who we had interest in also left the pub within a minute of our victim leaving the pub.

By dint of me going back to the Subway and the Arawa Bar we could establish that the guy in the bar had followed our victim down the road and although they had a conversation, we were unable to hear what was said as neither of the cameras had sound attached to them.

We, the Sarge and I, counted this as a victory. We did have footage of the guy following the victim down the road. And it was obvious that the victim was in no condition to drive. May be the guy had offered our victim a lift home. We did know that the victim's car had remained unmoved for a few days as it was now down at the main Copshop with the fingerprint lads having a go over it.

It was now well after midday, so we had our lunch and I settled down to making notes of everything about the case we had discovered so far. I often find that making notes about a case will help me put things like timing into perspective. At the end of my making notes, unfortunately I had nothing to add. Shortly after 3.00pm I headed out to my car and headed for Hamilton. I had the game and a few free beers to enjoy.

While making the trip to Hamilton I had the CD player going full belt. I may have been a child of the 1980's but I still preferred the music of the 70's. Around 4.30 I turned the music down. I'd made it as far as the Cambridge expressway and now I needed the Satnav or GPS to get me to the Boss's hotel.

I don't know about you, but I've got to the stage where I can usually only concentrate on one thing at a time and the music being turned right down is what I needed to get me to the Hotel.

That's when I noticed that the engine was running like a pig!

With the music turned up loud I'd never noticed it but with the music turned down I got the rough sounding engine loud and clear.

Pulling over, I got the handbook out. There was a service dealer on Anglesey St in Hamilton. I reprogrammed the GPS and headed in that direction. Obviously, I was right in the middle of the evening rush, but I got to the dealers about five minutes before they closed. The bloke there wasn't that helpful. Now I always tell the people I deal with that I am a Detective Sergeant. Often there are quite a few businesses that will give a discount to the Police Force. This bloke seemed even less inclined to help when I mentioned who I was. No, the mechanics were all about to go home. If I left it overnight, they, the Saturday morning crew, would probably take a look at it, if they weren't too busy.

I got on the phone to my Rotorua Dealership and explained that I had the vehicle in for it running a bit rough during the week. Fortunately the Rotorua guy asked me to hand the phone over to the Hamilton guy. I'd say there were a few words spoken that were not necessarily that kind or gentle. The Hamilton guy indicated that the Saturday morning crew would get onto my vehicle as the first job in the morning. He told me where to park it and buggered off!

Oh well, at least it would get sorted in the morning.

With that I rang the Boss and he said he was on his way to pick me up.

As far as the game went, I had a great time with my colleagues! The Chiefs won by about 15 points and there is a distinct possibility I may have over indulged, just a little bit! After the game I went back to the Boss's room and slept like a log. According to the Boss, I may have slept like a log with a chainsaw going full tilt for most of the night, but that is by the by.

Saturday

Over breakfast the next morning the Boss asked me how I was doing with my case, so I gave him all the details. He seemed pleased with my progress, and he also said he'd probably be back at Rotorua Nick by Tuesday or Wednesday. All in all I felt life was going pretty well. He dropped me off at the Service dealers and my car was all ready for me. It seems the HT lead was breaking down at the same spark plug the Rotorua guy had fixed for me. As I drove back to Rotorua, I did have a listen, but the engine was doing fine so I turned the music back on and the journey went by with no incidents.

I spent Saturday afternoon doing my laundry and rewatching the game from last night. It turned out to be a better game than I remembered, but then I didn't remember too much of it anyway!

Sunday

On Sunday I had a lie in and decided that I'd go to the Palace Tavern that night and have a word with the bar staff to see if anyone remembered anything from the previous Sunday night. I rang the Sarge to see if he fancied a pint. He said he'd come with me and invited me round to dinner before we went. I always enjoyed seeing him and his wife, and at least she'd have no chance to set me up with one of her mates. I'm something of a loner and I may let you into a little secret of mine later.

After we had dinner the two of us went to the Palace Tavern.

I'd timed it so we would get there about the same time as the victim last week.

I had a couple of photos I'd printed off, of the victim and of the guy we now considering as 'being of interest.'

I got the first pints in and had a look around the place. It probably hadn't changed that much in the last ten or so years. It was basically a cheap pub where the beer prices weren't that high. If anyone ever ordered a cocktail, the bar staff would have to look up the recipe in a book. It was that type of place.

The Sarge commented, "They'll be pleased to see the back of us. They've lost half a dozen customers since we walked in."

Quite a few of the remaining customers gave us a nod. It was probably because the Sarge had nicked them in the past or they felt, after a mental check, they weren't guilty and the Sarge would not nab them.

Either way, it felt like a local pub from back in England. It was a friendly place!

I asked the bartender if he remembered either of the two photos I had in my pocket and I showed them to him.

He replied, "Well the first one is the bloke you found in your rubbish bin last week. The second bloke, I've seen him in here. Hang on, he was here last Sunday night. Sat at the bar all night. I tried to talk to him, but he was an odd bloke to talk to."

I asked why he was an odd bloke.

The barman continued," Well, he reckons he was a book seller. A rep if you like. Said he was down to see the library girls and to see the two booksellers in town. Then he was off to Whakatane. Said he liked to get a head start on his run, so he came down from Auckland on the Sunday."

"So what was odd about him?"

"Well, I've never seen a rep that firstly uses this place as a watering hole and secondly, he was calloused on his hands and stains. A bit like grease. Like he did a manual job but was cracking on he was a rep for some reason. Weird really."

The Sarge was listening in and thanked the bartender for his input. Then he said, "I see you had the nobs last Sunday. Wasn't Jack Whitely in? the Insurance broker lad? Not often do you see him in this place."

"So that's who he was. Yeah, A posh bloke. Jeff Whiteley, you say. No, we never get his type slumming it."

The bartender walked away to serve someone and then he stopped and turned around, "That Whitely bloke. He was talking to your guy, the one in the picture, over in the doorway. They must have been speaking for at least a minute or so. Does that help?"

We thanked the bartender and then took our second pint over to a table and discussed our thoughts.

"So Whiteley came in here to have a chat with our guy," said the Sarge.

"Maybe it's time to go and have a chat with Jeff Whiteley."

"No," said the Sarge, " I'll go and have a word with him. He's my broker so I can drop in and have a chat. Might seem a bit more genuine!"

With that we supped our pints, and I dropped the Sarge off to his place in Huia St and I went home and watched a bit of" Elementary" but I dozed off and went to bed.

Chapter 4

M<u>onday</u>
In the morning, it was the turn of one of the new plods to go and get the coffee so I went straight in to the Sarge, and we waited for our coffee to be delivered.

We all got together and had our coffee and talked about updates since the last time we had spoken. I had the chance to talk about the game I'd been to. The two plods were talking about how they had firstly been bored being watched over by the ACI but once he had gone off and been seen by everybody, it got better. They'd gotten to speak to a couple of local lads, and they spent a fairly pleasant day with the locals telling them what was going on with the locals all speaking in Māori and explaining things to them. Overall, they'd had a reasonable day and were well pleased by the feed the women of the marae had put on for the gathering.

I brought them up to date with all the info I had gained from the CCTV footage I'd been looking at and the Sarge and I brought them up to speed with the conversation we'd had with the barman at the Palace Tavern last night.

The Sarge confirmed there was nothing of interest to the CIB that had happened over the weekend. That was unusual so I queried it. The Squaddies had all been roped off to go to a Drink Driving blitz in Tauranga so there was literally nothing to get excited about. I made a mental note to ring the desk at the main nick to check if there was anything that needed CIB coverage, but then I forgot about it.

Getting back to the murder, so our 'Person of interest" was a book rep down from Auckland. We all agreed that the person needed to be interviewed but we then stalled when we came up with ideas for how to track this lad down.

The best we could come up with was trawling through the phone book for Book wholesalers in Auckland and seeing if we could come up with anything. I of course handed this scut work off to the two new lads and left them to it.

For myself I had a few confidential informants I could go and interview. If that sounds a bit grand, trust me when I say I'm making it sound a bit grander than I was guilty of.

Let me explain. Once I became a Detective Sergeant, one of the first jobs I was landed with was being the newly named head of the vice squad. For the most part the vice squad work was telling the girls to always wear protection! You know what I mean so let's get past this part. When Covid hit, I was supposed to go and tell the girls to not do any business during Covid. These girls were doing this for a reason and that reason was money. So of course, they were going to keep doing it! About all I could say to them be sure and wear a bloody mask which would rather interfere with some of their activities. Again, I leave that to your own imagination.

Now for the guilty secret of mine. I slept with some of the girls!

There were only a few, three to be precise, but I'd had an incident with a WPC when I was a sergeant and the WPC thought it might help her promotion prospects if she was 'friendly' with a DS. It got a little messy, so I flagged it away. The three 'working girls I was friendly with were Tiff, Angel and Janet.

Tiff was of Chinese origin and Chinese girls were not noticeably 'well endowed' at the top of their bodies, so Tiff had gone under the knife and came out with a pair of C Cups. She was a lovely girl and I reckoned Tiff could have been named 'Stiff' because that's how she made me feel. Angel was also a working girl. part Māori, I think and she, like Tiff, were doing this kind of work to put bread on the table for their kids.

Janet was a different type of working girl. She was only doing it because she loved sex! Her hubby knew she was charging for it and somehow that made it all ok. Don't ask for a better reason because there isn't one. She loved the idea of sex with different blokes, and I was one of the lucky ones. Now, because I was effectively the 'Vice squad' It was sort of anticipated I would be on for freebies but that wasn't part of my thing. So I was maybe charged only half price and if I could get any useful info out of the girls, I'd give them a fair bit extra as a Criminal Informant. It sort of balanced itself out and there was generally a bit of info going on because, for some reason, blokes love to talk when they're naked. Don't ask me why but they do!

So I rang up my "CIs" to see if they had heard anything. I had to leave messages for all three of them, so they were either all busy or weren't available to chat.

While I had a half hour, I went back over the tapes we'd received from the Palace Tavern.

I couldn't figure it out, but I realised I had seen our 'person of interest" somewhere. I couldn't place him, but I reckoned that my Boss would want to review our progress when he returned. Perhaps he might remember the bloke.

It was approaching lunchtime, so I liaised with the Plods. They had drawn a blank. The guy did not work for any book wholesalers in Auckland. I suggested that after lunch they try the Wellington Wholesalers. The Sarge said he was going to drop in on Jeff Whiteley during his lunch hour.

I had a Subway for lunch and read the local papers. The local Daily Post was becoming more like the Weekend review. They were having to get more advertisers to subsidize flagging sales. Still they had a decent write-up on our case with lots of unanswered questions. At worst, we were all in the same boat!

The Sarge came in after his lunch and pulled me to one side.

"You'll never believe the yarn that Jeff Whiteley was trying to spin. Turns out he has a bit on the side and she's from the Palace. He went all quiet and shut his door on the receptionist. Said he'd value my discretion, but he has a girlfriend, and she hangs out at the Palace Tavern. Said he was only there to meet up with her."

I couldn't contain my chuckle and the Sarge gave me a poke in the ribs. "How did you keep a straight face while he was telling you this?"

The Sarge continued, "It wasn't bloody easy; I can tell you. But that takes the cake, as far as I am concerned. Jeff Whiteley having a bit on the side is a no go, not with his missus, and definitely not from the Palace. That's way too low on his social scheme to be a starter."

Just then the plods came back to me and had come up with nothing further, so I suggested they carry on and do all of the book wholesalers in the country. Just then I got a call from my Boss. He said they would be back in Rotorua Nick by lunchtime tomorrow. They could keep the accrued leave they had earned so they would be back tomorrow and take a week off in the school holidays. I'd be pleased to see the Boss back. The two DCs were coming right as well. Although I did have a bit of admiration for the two plods who were sticking to their tasks, as well.

At least, with the two DCs and the DI back I wouldn't have to cover the CIB duties all on my own.

Then I got a call from one of my "CI's", Tiff was saying she had something to show me. That was our code for nothing to really say but she had a free afternoon.

I went down to her place in Barnard Road and discussed a few things with her. As far as I am concerned it all comes down to swings and roundabouts. I don't mind going out for an evening to interview a client and it has to work both ways!

It was perhaps an hour or so later that I returned to Nick and checked up on all my paperwork to show the Boss tomorrow. Then I went home a tired and happy Chappy.

Tuesday

The two plods had come up with nothing from their phone around so we either had to assume the guy was a phony and the barman had been right or it just might be possible the guy worked out of Australia. It was too long a shot to think of ringing around Australia, so we assumed the guy was not a book seller and we were back to square one, other than we had a photo of him.

We assumed the tale he told the barman was false so that made it harder for us to track him down.

At 11.00 the Boss and the two DCs were back in the office, and they were welcomed back. The two new plods were a little confused that we were happy to see them back and it showed in their faces. The Boss straight away told them they would spit up and do work alongside the two DC's. Then he asked for a rundown on what had happened since he had been away, which was now more than two weeks!

Then he asked for an update on the cases we were running with. One was the murder victim, and the other case was the selling of drugs by the local 'Security team'.

We dealt with the Security men case first and then we moved to the murder victim in the rubbish skip at the back door of our office.

He was very businesslike the DI. He straight away said that Derek and Tim would pair up and that Dave and Dave would also be a pair. When I queried about the two plods being overdue to go back to the new Station and start out on patrol, the DI said that would not be an issue. I for one believed him. He has that sort of manner about him, does the DI.

"Right, Detective Sergeant. Give us all everything you know about the murder case. You've got the next half hour."

Surprisingly by the time we had explained the entirety of what we had come up with, we had pretty much covered a half hour.

Then the DI started to pepper us with questions. Oddly enough the questions were all relevant and questions Sarge and I had already discussed. I think the DI was pleased we were able to answer all of his questions with some authority and as the result of our research.

He was a little dismissive of the part about Jeff Whiteley. It seems that the DI knew Jeff from their occasional meetings at the Rotary club. I got the impression that the DI and the said businessman were not great friends.

<u>Wednesday</u>

It was Wednesday morning when I got the call from Janet. You may remember that Janet was one of my "CI" friends. She rang into the main Switchboard and was eventually put through to me. She started by calling me Detective Sergeant which sounded a little bit odd. Then she asked me to call round. When I offered to call round that afternoon, she insisted that I come there and then, That sounded a little odd, so I queried it. She wanted me to come round in my capacity as a member of the vice squad and she may have a crime to report.

I shot round to her place immediately. She rented a semi-permanent room at a motel in Malfroy Road, so it didn't take me long to get there.

When I got there, she let me in quickly. The room held quite a few memories for me, so I was wondering what she was going to tell me.

She asked a mate of hers who was in the bedroom to come through.

The mate was obviously in tears, so all my senses were on alert.

Janet started with, "I had a call last night from a bloke I've seen before. For whatever reason, I couldn't meet with him, so I gave Sharon a bell. She's always looking for a bit of work, so she was happy to fill in for me. When the bloke arrived, he was well pissed off that I wasn't here, so he started having a go at Sharon. By that time he was inside the room, and it just went downhill. Show him your back, Sharon."

Sharon lifted her shirt at the back, and she was covered in bruises where this bloke had given her a beating.

Janet then said, "Now show him your front. He's a regular of mine so don't be afraid. Go on!"

When she showed me her chest area, the marks were even worse than her back. I won't go into too much detail but it was obvious this bloke had inflicted damage by pinching her sensitive areas. Sharon was starting to cry again, so I told her to cover up and asked Janet for a cup of tea for us all to allow us to calm down and be objective.

"Janet, I need Sharon to tell me the story so shut up for five, would you?"

"Sharon. Give me as much detail as you feel comfortable with."

Sharon tried her best and every time Janet chipped in, I gave her the look to shut up!

We got through her story which included quite a bit of sobbing.

Basically the bloke had expected to see Janet and had gone berko when Sharon turned up at the motel door stripped down to her underwear. He'd come inside and then started beating on Sharon, demanding to know how to get hold of Janet. Okay I could see where a bloke might have a fetish for a certain girl, but this was going too far.

Then he had forced her to have a drink of something and Sharon had gone quite woozy. Even though she was mostly out of it, she knew she had to keep Janet away from this idiot. Then the beating began, and he forced her to have sex. Even though it was with a hooker it would still sound like nonconsensual sex so now I had the issue of asking Sharon if she would press charges and between her and Janet, I got agreement that Sharon would press charges.

I joked and said it would be great if we had any video of it.

That was the time Janet turned sheepish and said that there was a video. Every one of her clients was videoed and thought the tape only had eight hours on it, it would show the actual offense taking place.

It suddenly dawned on me that I might have appeared in one of her videos, but I had the sense to not ask about that until Janet and I were next alone!

Janet went and got the video out of the mirror at the end of the bed. She dug something out of her purse and then took out her laptop and within a minute we were watching a video of last night and the beating that Sharon took.

It might just be a man thing but it took a minute or more before I realised that the bloke in the video was also the same guy as our "Person of interest" in the murder case I was working on. During the ongoing video I mentioned this to the two girls and then Janet shrieked, "That Prick was here to do me harm! Maybe he was out to do me in."

Suddenly, the whole complexity of the situation started to make sense to me. I asked the girls to give me the video to take down to the station. I had a whole mess of thoughts running through my head. Not the least of which was that I may have appeared in one of Janet's videos! That would be embarrassing, to say the least!

Janet followed me out to my car and said, "Seeing those vids is a bit of a turn on for Eric (Her husband) but I swear I never let him look at one of my specials, and that includes you."

Feeling only slightly mollified I went back to the Station. There I spoke to the Sarge and to the Boss. We got into the computer and asked the DC's and the two plods to give us a bit of privacy.

We'd only got a couple of minutes into the video when the Sarge spotted that was our 'Man on Interest' in the video. Within a couple of more minutes, the Boss was saying, "Sarge, you're right, this is our guy!"

Now, both the Boss and I thought we knew our suspect but could not work out from where we had met him. The Boss and I also knew we had a secondary case of sexual assault and even drugging the victim if we couldn't make the murder charge stick.

The Boss turned away and then turned back," I never forget a face. You get that video from the Palace Tavern you got hold of and then come and see me in my office."

I dug out the video of our suspect and went to the Boss's office. The Boss also called for the Sarge to come into his office as well.

The Boss was busy tapping away at his computer.

Then he said, "Got the bastard! Detective Sergeant cast your mind back to the weekend. Where did you go?"

"At the weekend I came up to the game with you and your mates from Hamilton. Don't tell me he was at the game. I'm not surprised I didn't clock him."

"Nope," said the Boss

"He was in the corporate box drinking with you and me?"

"Nope!" I hated it when I was asked to play twenty questions.

"How about this bloke?" said the Boss and turned round his computer monitor so it faced me.

Straight away I knew the Boss was on the button.

The Sarge said, "Well that's why I didn't know him. Only you and the DS would have spoken to him.

"So who is this bloke?" I was still confused.

The Sarge spoke first while the Boss looked smug. "Well from this website I'd say you met him when your motor was giving you problems on Friday Night. This is the Dealer's place from Hamilton, and he was one of the mechanics. Did he work on your car?"

"No he didn't and as soon as I said I was with the Police at Rotorua, He didn't want to have anything to do with me. Told me to leave it there and he'd get the lads to look at it in the morning. No wonder if this is our bloke, he wanted to get away from me!"

The Boss continued to look smug, but I had to admit that the Boss had a better memory for faces than I did. The Boss gave me his final shot, "Trust me, if they're not a villain yet, it's only a matter of time!"

Given that he worked in Hamilton it did present us with a few minor problems. The Boss got on to the phone and spoke to his opposite number in Hamilton. I could hear his conversation.

He was asking the Hamilton lads to give him a rundown on the guy at the garage. Previous work; any work with the Army or armed forces; any history of violence etc. The Boss also asked him to call round to the garage and make sure he was still there. As the Boss had a few mates in

Hamilton Nick there was a quick response. This guy had a history of violence in the Army and a few disciplinary marks against him, which resulted in him being 'let go' from the Army. He was a good mechanic so had easily got a job. In addition he had a record of being a bit handy with his fists in a couple of confrontations when he was a bouncer for a Hamilton nightclub which had resulted in him being released from his job as a bouncer. As a plus the Hamilton lads also sent a copy of the dealer's website which showed him as a mechanic, and he'd been with that firm for over twelve months. Also we discovered his name, which was Carl Jeffries. We already had the website, but it was a measure of the regard they had for the Boss that they went to so much trouble for him.

The Boss stuck his neck out and asked the locals to go and pick him up and we would be there within a couple of hours to interview him.

With that, the Boss and I were on our way to Hamilton along with the video evidence from the working girls and the Palace Tavern.

By the time we arrived at the Hamilton Nick, Carl, our 'person of interest' had become withdrawn and a little surly.

We showed him the evidence from the working girls first. He tried to deny it but there was ample evidence just from his back. The silly sod had a big eagle tattooed on his back, so it wasn't a hard case to prove. Why do they all do that? Go with the big eagle on their back? Is it a soldier thing? He finally admitted he had been there in Rotorua. He also admitted he had gone to see Janet and was 'disappointed' when she had not shown up.

He wasn't going anywhere so the Boss and I had a quick chat. We decided to leave him without knowing he was also a suspect in the murder case. He went off to Waikeria Prison and we drove back to Rotorua, feeling just a little pleased with ourselves!

It was a little after 6.00pm when we got back to Rotorua.

When we got back, I phoned Sharon and I also phoned Janet, to let them both know we had the offender locked up. Janet was especially pleased as she was now convinced that the guy from Hamilton had come to do her no good. I also arranged to meet Janet and Sharon at Janet's place for a photo ID for the perp. I just printed off the five faces of the mechanics from the dealership and presented them to both girls. Janet was always trying to be helpful but, in the end, I had to shut her out so that Sharon could identify the photo. Then I asked Sharon to go out of the bedroom so Janet could identify the suspect. There were no problems once I had the logistics sorted out and both of the girls easily identified Carl Jeffries as the one who had visited them. As a final note Janet said she also had a camera outside her place so she could get the bloke's car and possible number plates of her visitors

This concerned me a little bit. Why was she hanging on to vehicles and number plates. Was she doing a bit of blackmail? For some reason, that automatically occurred to me. I made a mental note to check her on that point when I next saw her. At the same time, it occurred to me that if she had the number plate of the murderer's motor, we may be able to get him going around to the back of our temporary office. I rang her back and shot round to grab the exterior video footage. I never mentioned my suspicions to her about blackmail. I'd wait for a quiet moment before I broached that subject.

Thursday

Well we did identify the guy's number plate and his motor which was a dark blue pickup, A Ute type thing. Quite a modern one. It was one of the cheaper Chinese models that they were trying to break into the NZ market with. Maybe I'd have a look at these cheaper jobs the next time I was looking for a new car. If a mechanic says they were alright, they can't be that bad.

I sent two of the lads out to see if we could get any footage from the likely paths they may have taken on the way round to the back of our office.

I didn't have that much hope. Most security cameras today have a twenty-four-hour reel of tape. That means when you get to the end of twenty-four hours it deletes what you have recorded, and it records over the tape again. However I was being too pessimistic. The chemist opposite the Courthouse had a tape that went onto their hard drive and the library cameras were the same!

When I looked at the camera footage, I could only get the side on view of the dark blue Ute on both of the cameras but that did at least put the vehicle in our vicinity!

I have to be honest that going up to interview our suspect was a real pain as he was held in Waikeria which is outside of Te Awamutu. It was a good hour or so to go and see him and then we had the return trip.

He'd had a go at getting bail from the Hamilton Court, but we strenuously opposed any bail, so they banged him back inside. We had the tape from Janet as a backup, but it wasn't needed once we revealed there was photographic evidence to place the accused at the scene of the assault and drugging. He was driven straight back to Waikeria Prison. At least if he was banged up in there our two working girls were safe! Don't be too hard on our working girls. They provide a necessary service and if we didn't have them there'd probably be more sexual assaults on the books.

Right! Our next job was to connect the murder to this guy.

The Boss decided on a bold strategy for this.

On Thursday, after lunch we were both headed up to see Carl Jeffries at Waikeria.

Sitting down with the accused the Boss casually slipped in that "We know about Jeff Whiteley".

At first the accused looked a little crestfallen. Then he brightened and said, "What do you know about this Jeff Whiteley, then?"

I knew damn well that we were bluffing but the bugger had turned it all around and called our bluff!

The Boss dismissed his query and went back to discussing the sexual assault case. It was a pity as I might have pushed a little harder, but the Boss was now the guy in charge of the investigation.

Our accused reluctantly agreed to most aspects of our investigation and realised he'd be up for anything from five years inside to maybe as long as twelve years for the sexual assault and drugging case. It didn't seem to faze him that much. Our next step was to get him back to court and for the courts to determine when a date could be set down for trial. It would have to be held at Rotorua and the Boss and I knew we'd be lucky to get a trial date inside three months. But at least the accused was locked up and out of harm's way while he was waiting for a trial.

On the drive back to Rotorua we talked about what our next steps should be.

For a while we discussed whether it was a good idea to have a go at Jeff Whiteley. The Boss seemed a little reluctant to call in Whiteley for an interview. He reckoned they had something of a history at Rotary and it might be awkward for the duration of the interview. I volunteered my services and the Boss reluctantly agreed to it.

That took good care of Thursday and when we got to the station, I went off home to my place and had a quiet night in with a few more episodes of "Elementary".

Friday

By the time the next morning came round, I was bright and early and nearly beat the Sarge in. One of the plods went over for the coffee and we went over our summary for the day over our coffees. The Sarge had a few items from the Squaddies' previous night's visits. The Boss simply said the new guys and the DC's would handle them. I did like it when the Boss had his teeth into a new case, and he would delegate all other sundries to the new lads.

Dave and Dave, (the DC and the new Plod) were having a little bit of success with their investigation into the drugs being supplied to the local homeless. It seemed they could reasonably foretell when the locals went over to the Tauranga boys to get their top up of supplies.

If they could set up an intercept of the vehicle on its return trip, fully loaded, they could probably create an arrest.

The Boss authorised them to get it organised and they planned the sting for Friday and or Saturday. This would basically involve them parking up at the layby on the right-hand side of the road and getting a few license plate numbers to look out for.

As for our other major case, the sexual assault and the murder, the Boss told the lads what had happened at Waikeria, yesterday.

Opinion was divided about whether we should bring in Jeff Whiteley for questioning. The Sarge had the most decisive voice when he said we should get the bugger in. He gave no credence to Jeff's claim he was having a bit on the side.

Having discussed our two, or three, major cases we firstly set out to organise the intercept of the drugs coming in from Tauranga. It would need to be an all-hands-on deck situation. One car would park at the layby and the other car would park as if they were going on the river rides at Okawa Bay. If the first car couldn't get the druggies to stop, the other lads could force a roadblock on the Okawa Bay stretch, at the bridge.

For our main investigation we would ask Jeff Whiteley to call into our office on the assumption he was popping in to see the Sarge about his new boat.

With all of the planning underway, the Sarge rang Jeff and asked him to call around to his office so he could talk further about the boat he was planning to buy. From the Sarge's end of the phone call I worked out that Jeff would be here around 11.30.

The Sarge asked if he could sit in the interview and the Boss agreed so it was all going to plan.

When Jeff arrived, the Sarge and I took him into the interview room.

Jeff was a little surprised but didn't object.

I opened the discussion, "Jeff, you went to the Palace Tavern a week ago on Sunday night. Why were you there?"

With Sarge's nod, Jeff explained that he would rely on our discretion, but he had been to see a young lady he was friendly with.

I continued, "That sounds a bit odd Jeff. Because we have footage of the bar around the time you went in and there were no women in the bar."

Okay, I was bluffing, but he didn't need to know that.

Jeff went a bit red in the face and said, "Er no. She was a little late getting there. She didn't arrive until a bit later."

So I continued, "Jeff, you don't mind if I call you Jeff, do you?"

Jeff was looking a little less like a confident Insurance bloke by this point.

"No er... no, that's fine."

I think it was the Boss who told me that trick. If you call them by their first name it gives them a bit of pain. It almost feels like you are invading their space.

"Okay Jeff. It turns out your bird didn't arrive, and you would have left within maybe five minutes, maybe ten minutes?"

"Oh, you mean the Sunday night about a week ago. No, no. The stupid tart was a no show. Now I remember. I probably hung around for ten minutes and I went home."

It was nice when a suspect was on the hook, and you could see them squirming around.

"So, Jeff. It appears you had a conversation with this fellow. What did you talk about?" I showed him the photo we had of the suspect in the murder and the sexual assault case.

"Oh, that bloke. That's right. He asked me where the toilets were. That was about it, really."

"That's a bit odd, Jeff. We have a witness that says you spoke to this bloke for about five or ten minutes. I should add that this person is helping us with our enquiries concerning a sexual assault incident."

At the mention of a sexual assault incident, you could almost see Jeff's brain going through several stages. Firstly he was wondering if this guy had done something sexual to the victim. Then there was the realization that we might be asking whether or not Jeff had anything to do with the sexual assault. You could almost see Jeff's face as he realised he might be implicated with something just a little inappropriate.

"Well I had nothing to do with anything like that!"

I knew which way this conversation was going. Jeff was about to lawyer up, which nicely led me to my final question. "So what were you saying to this bloke then, Jeff?"

This, of course, led to Jeff asking for his lawyer. Along with protestations that we shouldn't be asking these types of questions to a guy and did we know he went to Rotary with my Boss etc.

While we didn't have enough to hold him, we did have enough to make him hang on and speak to his lawyer. When the lawyer arrived, we left them alone for a minute or two and then the Sarge and I went back in to speak to them.

The lawyer was quick to shut us up.

" If you have anything to accuse my client of, please let us get on with it. If not, I will advise my client to say nothing more to you and we shall leave."

The lawyer's name was Ian Clegg.

"Good heavens no, Ian. We were just going through the questioning of a possible witness to an incident last week. Jeff has already told us he was there to meet a lady friend. Perhaps we could speak again. Obviously, it would be probably advisable for you to be present, so we'll speak again when you are available, or perhaps one of your colleagues?"

With that we invited Jeff and his lawyer to leave the interview. It was quite obvious that the lawyer wasn't going for the alibi that Jeff was at the Palace Tavern to meet his bird. Maybe they'd have a conversation back at Jeff's office to discuss what was really going on.

All in all, a good morning's work!

Because we were only in temporary accommodation at the Nick, we didn't have one of those rooms adjacent to the interview room where the other guys could listen in to the conversation. You know, like they have in the American series, a room off to the side with a one-way mirror in it.

Still I was quite happy with how the conversation went.

The Sarge, once he'd escorted Jeff and his lawyer out, came back into the CIB room and spoke.

"I don't know why he was at the Palace Tavern that night, but he's definitely guilty of something."

In my opinion I reckoned he was there to finger the victim, but I was probably clutching at straws to make my case a better fit.

The Boss entered the room at that point. He'd been away doing something else. I think he was having his regular weekly meeting with the ACI.

"So, how did you get on?" asked the Boss.

The Sarge replied that we'd got him to admit the girlfriend's story was probably a phony but then he'd lawyered up, so we hadn't pushed it too far.

The Sarge reckoned we should give him or the suspect in Waikeria Prison a chance to rat on the co-conspirator.

Given that was the best idea we had, the Boss and I decided to head back to Waikeria, and we'd let the Sarge pop in on Jeff Whiteley and make him the offer.

With that, we had our lunch and then headed off to Waikeria and the Sarge dropped in on Jeff. Just to chew the fat, as it were.

Once we had met with Carl again at Waikeria we offered him the deal. At first, he was adamant that he wouldn't be a part of anything that helped the cops!

Then the Boss chipped in with, "That sounds a bit stupid, Carl! We're already making the same offer to the bloke we reckon is your co-conspirator. Whichever one of you turns first, well I reckon it might add another year or two to your sentence to whichever one doesn't help us in our investigation. Let's face it. You're already up for perhaps a ten to fifteen term. With murder as well I reckon, we can almost make that a maximum term. What do you reckon, 25 to life? Wouldn't you say, Detective Sergeant?"

I nodded as I didn't want to spoil the Boss's flow.

Carl burst in with, " You haven't got me for no murder!"

The Boss continued as if Carl had not interrupted.

" So you were down in Rotorua on the Sunday night. Don't really know why, but we've got you in the pub. You give a blatantly false lie about why you were there. You meet your contact who fingers the mark for you. You slip him a mickey so he's pretty legless when you get him outside. We've got CCTV footage of you offering to drive him home and then we've got you parking up at the back of our place. We also know you've got a temper. Pinning the murder on you is our next job but even if we don't, you're still up for the rape and sexual assault of the girl. Gotta say, Carl, it's not looking good for you at this point. I tell you what, we'll let you think about for a day or two. If we don't hear from you, we'll just assume you're happy to take the rap for everything. Come on Detective Sergeant, let's get back to Rotorua. Perhaps the other bloke will be smarter and help us."

With that we both got up to leave. Carl said, "Let me think about it for a day and I might get back to you."

The Boss said nothing, so I followed his lead and carried on out of the visitor's room.

The Boss was quite happy once we'd gotten outside. "I'd say he's seventy percent round to our way of thinking."

By the time we got back to Rotorua it was getting towards five o'clock, so we had a brief meeting with the Sarge.

He told us that he'd 'dropped' in on Jeff Whiteley and apologised.

It had, supposedly, completely taken him by surprise when I had ushered him and the Sarge into the interview room and my line of questioning had further taken him aback. This was why Jeff said he had been so quiet during the interview.

The Sarge then suggested that if Jeff knew anything about the situation, he would advise Jeff to get into a plea deal with me as I had a reputation for worrying things like a dog with a bone once I had my teeth into something. I thought the Sarge had done quite well by still purporting a supposed friendship with Jeff.

With that I went home and cooked myself some tea. When I sat, I realised I'd finished the series of "Elementary" so now I'd have to dig out a new DVD series. It was a shame because I quite liked the series and now, I'd have to decide on a new programme to watch. Maybe I'll have a go at this TVNZ+ thing I'd been hearing so much about.

Chapter 5

S<u>aturday</u>

I woke up bright and early and was into the office at 7.30. The girl at the library café was surprised to see me as we usually didn't cover a Saturday. There were a few small items for the CIB to work with. A robbery and a sexual assault. The Boss was adamant he wanted the newer guys to handle new cases. He said he didn't want me distracted when we were so close to getting one over the line. He set me to work on the paperwork for Carl Jeffries. There wasn't that much I could do but I made myself look busy until the new lads came back from their visits.

We were set to do the drug run ambush today. The Boss would stay at the office, and I would go out with one of the cars. It was decided that I would go in the car that was to be parked at the layby. Then Dave and Dave would take the Okawa Bay bridge. It was probably getting close to 11.00 before we set out for the layby. We went out to the planned positions and waited. Finally, it would have been around four o'clock we saw one of the suspect cars drive past. We were straight out and onto its tail.

It wasn't speeding or anything. There were two guys in the seats of the car we were following so we were fairly confident that we could match them with the three of us in our car. We followed them for perhaps a kilometer more before we pulled them over.

I knew something was wrong when I stepped out of the car. The two guys were immediately out of the car and lighting up a cigarette each. They were too calm!

We'd drawn weapons for this bust, so we drew our weapons and approached them. They held their hands up, but they didn't seem too concerned.

When I asked their permission to search the vehicle they readily agreed and acted as if they wondered why on earth, we would want to search their vehicle.

Obviously, we gave their car a good search. Equally obviously, we found absolutely nothing!

After about ten minutes of us searching and these guys are grinning at us, we were forced to let them go.

As they drove off, we saw the other detective's car approaching us, so we flagged them over.

We had drawn a blank with the search and it hinted that they might have got a tip off and they were just going over for a nice ride to Tauranga and back. Probably, just to piss us off!

We headed home and I rang the Boss to tell him the drug bust was a no go. He wasn't too disappointed and told me to have a good weekend and he'd see me on Monday. Then he corrected himself and told us to take Monday off. We'd had a success or two this week and we deserved an extra day away from the Office.

I didn't have anything to do on Monday, so I planned a lazy day. Perhaps go and see Janet if she feels up to it.

On Sunday I had a lazy day and mostly watched golf and anything else they were showing on Sky Sports. On Monday I started with a reminder to myself to do something useful. I always felt like that after I had had a lazy day.

I started with tidying up my unit and then I ended up with mowing my lawns. That brought lunchtime up fairly well, so I made myself some lunch and then wondered about ringing Janet up.

I took a punt and rang her. Ostensibly it was just to see how she was doing, but she seemed up for it so went around to the motel on Malfroy Road.

It was always fun when we got down to doing what she does best. Once we got to the 'resting stage' I didn't think it was too appropriate to mention my thoughts on the blackmail thing, so I kept my mouth shut.

It was just as well. She said she always felt a bit more relaxed knowing I was looking out for her. I should add that at this time, we were both naked, so it was snuggling down under the covers time. It was nice.

Then she added that Sharon was having second thoughts about appearing as a witness against the accused. I suggested that without Sharon we wouldn't have a case unless the idiot pleaded guilty. We er.. carried on and then I went home to have a think about life and the case and anything else I could come up with.

<u>Tuesday</u>

I rolled into work and got a smart remark from the Sarge about how nice it must be for the fancy pants in civvies to take a day off when they wanted. I ignored it as I knew the Sarge was probably just joking. Once we had our coffee delivered, we all sat round in the CIB room and discussed what had gone down on Friday and Saturday. By common agreement we decided that it would be a complete waste of time to repeat last Saturday's efforts as the gangs would be expecting this.

I reckoned there had been leak but the Boss reckoned the only person he had mentioned it to was the Acting Chief Inspector at their weekly meeting. So that was a no go!

It was Derek Besant who came up with the idea.

He said, "Hey Boss, who do the homeless people from the hotels call when they have an issue going on?"

The Boss replied with, "Not our problem. If they have an issue, they get on to Jacko's security team and they deal with it. Why?"

Jacko was the head of the security team that was, to our thoughts, supplying them with drugs and the like.

Derek continued, "Well if we got on to the issue first, we'd be able to keep a closer eye on things at the motels, wouldn't we? Maybe get a better picture of what's going on?"

The Boss looked at Derek. I thought it was definitely something we could think about. The Boss continued, "That's a brilliant idea. I'd need to get the squad cars involved but it's a definite starter!"

The talk continued with ideas on how to get on top of the drug suppliers. It was a very positive meeting. Then the Boss and the Sarge and I had a separate meeting.

The Boss said, "It won't be easy selling it to the patrol lads, but I'll have a go tomorrow morning before they go out on patrol."

I reckoned the Boss should take the Sarge with him as he still held quite a bit of pull over the road. The Boss agreed, over the Sarge's objections, so that was a done deal. We had to tell the ACI what we were doing so that was also left to the Boss as it would mean extra work for the patrol lads.

All in all, I reckoned that we were at an advantage over the drug suppliers, and they couldn't do anything to stop us.

The next couple of days passed quickly. The Boss went and talked to the patrol lads, and they were up for it. Anything to stop the drug suppliers was a bonus for the patrol lads. A few suggestions came out of that meeting. One of the issues was that the suppliers were all fairly much established with the Black Power Mob. This was a surprise for the Boss as he didn't think the Black Power had much of a finger in Rotorua's Crime stats. Another idea was that the Boss should be talking to the motel owners or managers and telling them to call the cops direct if they had any idea there was a barney going on at their motel. All in all it was a very positive meeting. And so was the meeting with the ACI, which surprised me a little. The ACI was all for it as he was getting some flak from the Council. It seems that there had been a programme on the Sunday evening that mentioned the issues that Rotorua was having with the homeless being put up in motels. Jacko's security firm were alluded to as having an undue influence over the homeless and there were several instances where the TV programme questioned how on earth did some of the so-called security men ever get past the security scrutiny that any security guy had to undergo. There was a brief allusion to the cops being involved but it was only mentioned once, and I think that was just to spread a bit of the blame. We all knew the cops were too busy to be involved in any way!

Chapter 6

F<u>riday</u>

On Friday morning we received a call from Carl Jeffries, our suspect for the murder case, who was in Waikeria. He said he'd like to have a chat with us.

Naturally, the Boss and I were happy to go over to Waikeria and have a chat with him.

When we got there, Carl was looking quite confident, a bit too confident if you ask me.

After pleasantries were exchanged, Carl got right down to it.

"Okay, I might be willing to do a deal with you blokes but first I want to know what you know so I can make my decision."

The Boss replied with, "Well we've got you bang to rights with the sexual assault case, and the drugging of the victim."

Carl wanted more. "Yeah, but you're trying to pin a murder on me as well. What have you got on that?"

I was initially taken aback but the Boss was right onto it, fortunately.

The Boss replied with, "We've got you in the pub, we've got you walking outside with the victim, we've got you offering the victim a ride in your car because he could barely walk straight, probably because you gave him something in his drink."

Carl looked a little surprised and he nodded that yes, he might have doctored the victim's drink.

The Boss continued, "We've got you going round to the library, and we've got you parking your nice blue motor just down the road from the library. And we've also got you for the sexual assault and the drugging of the girl you beat up and raped."

Carl looked a little shocked that we had so much on him. I was trying hard not to look shocked that a lot of what the Boss was saying was supposition. We didn't really have him parking at the library and beyond that we were taking a punt.

Carl thought about what we had said and then he came out with, "I'll tell you what I'll do. You get me a guarantee that I will only get a max of fifteen years and I'll give you three murders, no make that four murders and three times I gave a few blokes a good hiding. Now I want that in writing, and I'll give you all the details you will want. I'll leave it with you lads to get that in writing and then we'll talk, maybe!"

With that he signaled to the prison warden that he was done talking. He got up and said "Remember, I want it in writing. No more than 15 years total inside and then I'm out. Well it looks like you've got something to keep you busy over the next few days. I'll see you next week, maybe. Cheers, lads"

Then he walked off to his cell leaving the Boss and me gob smacked.

For a second, we struggled with what to say, then I was the first to speak.

"He's just offered us three or four murders and a few beatings and in return he only gets fifteen years. Is it doable? Him getting away with only fifteen?"

The Boss replied, "It might be doable, don't forget he has the drugging and sex assault as a topper. I think it might be doable, but it depends what mood we get from the Crown Prosecutor. Come on. Let's head home and we'll call in to the Crown Prosecutor's office on the way."

On the way back I was immersed in my own thoughts. Were the four murders committed in Rotorua? Let's forget the beatings for the time being. How did Jeff Whiteley fit into all of this? Why was Carl Jeffries based in Hamilton and doing his dirty deals in Rotorua? I didn't realise how deep in thought I was until the Boss said we were back in Rotorua, and we should go and see the CP at his office.

The CP, or Crown Prosecutor, had his own law firm full of Barristers and Solicitors on Arawa St. We parked up the road in the only spot available and walked into his reception. Within a few minutes we were sat down in front of the CP and explained our deal, perhaps it was our predicament rather than our deal?

The CP was initially inclined to say no. For a series of murders such as four, the penalty would start at twenty years and then go up. Was this guy a serial killer? Was he acting on his own? A member of a gang? Was he doing it for money? After a few minutes of talking by the Boss, and me chipping in a word or two here and there, the CP agreed to think about it over the weekend and get back to us on the Monday.

It was now after 4.00 so we went back to the Nick and filled in the Sarge. He was blown away!

His first thought was that we hadn't had four murders in the last few years. Well. Not four where the accused had not been found. He could comfortably imagine a few beatings that might fit the description. Anyway, we were now waiting on the CP to decide whether we could offer the suspect a deal. I went home and decided to have a lazy weekend. Or so I thought!

It was around midday when I got a call from the Boss. Apparently an inmate in Waikeria had taken exception to something Carl Jefferies had said or done and tried to knife him with a hand-made blade. What the guy hadn't realized was that Carl was ex-army and quite capable of defending himself. Carl had suffered a cut to the back of his hand but the other guy was in the hospital fighting for his life. There were plenty of onlookers to support Carl's 'innocence'.

The second call I received was also from the Boss, suggesting we get over to Waikeria smartish before Carl had any other 'incidents' to deal with.

Weekends come and weekends go, and I had just had an extra day off the previous weekend so I couldn't really complain about losing the Sunday afternoon. I went round to pick the Boss up and we went off to Waikeria.

I think the Boss might have been a little' the worse for wear' as he insisted that I drive over. Normally we would go in his BMW but today we were slumming it in my Mitsubishi SUV.

The Boss was quiet as we drove. He wondered if anyone at Waikeria could have been tempted to have a go at Carl, perhaps due to some 'outside' influence. As the two of us and the Sarge were the only ones who were aware of the new situation, we discarded that theory and then wondered if Carl had been too mouthy to a few of the other residents. Either way we had to get Carl into a separate room away from the other inmates.

When we got to see Carl, he was surprised to see us. Yes, there had been an incident over lunch, but there were plenty of witnesses who would testify that Carl was the innocent party. As a matter of fact it had done Carl's reputation, inside, a power of good. Now Carl was seen as a player in the greater hierarchy of things inside and not a bloke to be trifled with!

He did ask if we arranged to see the adjutant, by that I assumed he meant the CP as this was in civvy life. I told him we had already seen the Crown Prosecutor and it was up to him. We'd probably know by Monday. I didn't want to seem too keen with Carl.

Driving back, the Boss reckoned I'd handled things quite well, especially not seeming too keen with Carl. Then he went into a spiel about negotiating tactics. Yes, I reckon the Boss might have had a few when I picked him up.

Chapter 7

<u>M</u><u>onday</u>
Going into the nick on Monday, I was able to update the Sarge on Sunday's activities, including the Boss being a little tipsy. Evidently the Boss was known for having a few at the weekend. Not my problem to deal with.

The Sarge filled me in on everything that had happened in Rotorua that required our attention. Once I had my coffee, I was better equipped to deal with it all. The criminal fraternity had a field day over the weekend - two domestic assaults, one/possibly two cases of GBH, two burglaries, (commercial) and two domestic burglaries.

When I looked at the actual crimes, I was better pleased. With both domestic burglaries the victim had returned during the event and the two people who had committed the GBH had actually done it on the two burglars. I felt I should handle this one as I could probably get the two accused to admit what and why these events had occurred. The Boss handed the rest of the cases off to the DCs and their new partners. The Boss took on one of the commercial burglaries with the proviso that he would take on the other one if the first one didn't take too long.

It was just before 9.30 in the morning when I got the call from the CP on my cellphone. The Crown Prosecutor was wondering if our Carl would wear a maximum of twenty years. I said I'd see and left the CP to his court appearance.

The Boss wandered in around 10'o'clock and I was in just a few minutes later. I told him what the CP had suggested. The Boss reckoned I should go back and say that the deal was fifteen years or nothing. I said I'd get onto it later.

It turns out that Derek's idea of the patrol cars turning up at the motels was paying dividends. There had been three incidents over the weekend and as a result we had one guy banged up for possession with intent to supply. When they searched his car, he had twenty-two bags of crystal meth and fourteen baggies of wacky baccy. It was all there in the centre console of his motor. Absolutely no intention to hide what he was up to. Amazing, really, that they think they can deal this stuff without any consequences. There was a brief debate on whether the Squaddies or the CIB should process this case. The Boss reckoned the Squaddies could handle this one and they needed a few successes. The downside of the good news was that a lot of druggies were now desperate for their fix. The further downside was that there were a few more 'ladies of the night' on the streets.

I can deal with that if we're putting the dealers inside.

Later, I had the two DC's, and the two plods go over their cases that they had dug out last week to see if we could spot any of the murders that our lad in Waikeria was owning up to.

The Boss was going over the incidents over the weekend and straightway zoomed in to the case of the guy selling drugs. He said out loud, to no one in particular, "This is a good collar. Well done to the guy who came up with this one."

Then he went over the road to the cells to have a word with this guy. I reckon he was trying to turn him to our side.

By now I was at something of a loose end. I had no active cases coming across my desk and I was waiting to speak to the CP about our murder case. The Sarge came up to have a quiet word with me.

"What are we going to do about Jeff Whiteley? Do we go round and pull him in? or do we let him hang for a while. If your bloke in Waikeria is going to go Queen's evidence. Oh no, I have to stop saying that. If your bloke is turning King's evidence, how do we handle Jeff?"

I really didn't know how the Boss was going with him. It seemed they knew each other from Rotary but I'd got the impression they weren't very big mates. I told the Sarge I would bring it up with the Boss when he returned.

I rang the CP as I was anxious to get it over with. As luck would have it, he was back in his office and in a good mood. The case he had been working on was supposed to go for three days and the guy being charged had pleaded guilty within five minutes of the case opening. The CP had already booked the three days out, so he was going to get paid anyway. I'm sure he was in a great mood. I relayed that the deal was only for a maximum of fifteen years and like a trooper he rolled over and said he would have to get 15 years as a minimum so if he misbehaved or got violent, he might be there for longer. If that was acceptable, he'd put it in writing, and we'd get it before five o'clock that night.

I have to say I was well chuffed. I also wanted to get over to Waikeria and get him to talk about these other murders he'd spoken about.

When the Boss returned, I told him about my conversation with the CP and he was delighted. He'd had a go with the drug seller this morning and that was a no go. It seems that Black Power sees doing time in prison as something of a rite of passage. So we were now waiting for the CP to send over the letter and then we could go up to Waikeria.

Unfortunately the letter did not arrive until after 4.00 o'clock so we decided to head over to the prison the following morning.

That afternoon, for something to do I went to View Road to see Ronnie, the head of the Mongrel Mob.

Ronnie was pleased to see me and as he was making himself a fresh cup of tea we sat down and talked. Ronnie reckoned we were doing a 'load' for his business. With the rival Black Power wondering who was going to be there at the hotels and motels he reckoned they were increasing their turnover in drugs due to the uncertainty. Not that the Mob were admitting being a party to dealing in drugs, but my Bosses should put me on commission for the extra business they were getting.

I probably spent a half hour with Ronnie and it must have been around five o'clock when I left him and headed straight for home.

Tuesday

The next morning, bright and early, we headed back to Waikeria. It was now getting to the stage where I was becoming quite familiar with the journey, so I was 'otherwise occupied' when the Boss was driving over. I could tell that the Boss was also deep in thought as we travelled so it was a quiet trip over.

Once we got to the prison we were let in, and the guards let us use one of their interview rooms.

Then they brought Carl into the room. They gestured to us to see if we wanted Carl to be handcuffed but we were happy that if he was unchained, his speech might also be a bit more relaxed.

The Boss gave Carl the letter and he seemed quite happy with it. He asked for a copy for himself and then he co signed the letter before saying," So, where would you like to start, lads?"

The Boss wanted to make it a bit more formal, so he'd brought over a video camera he'd borrowed from the main station over the road to keep a record of what everyone was saying. This would form the basis of Carl's confession and he would have to sign that.

The Boss opened the recording by saying that this was a formal interview between Carl Jonathan Jeffries and the two interviewing officers who he then mentioned by name and rank. He then went on to say that the informant and accused had asked for a plea deal with the Rotorua Crown Prosecutor which had been granted in return for the accused pleading guilty to four murders and three counts of Grievous Bodily Harm. He looked over at me and I had to shrug my shoulders as I didn't have much of a clue either as to what to say. I mentioned the sexual assault case, but the Boss let it slide.

Then he indicated that I would be leading the interview while he listened. I do wish he'd mentioned this in the drive over, but as it was my case, I suppose it was for me to lead the questioning.

Carl was happy to get things started and asked, "So where would you lads like me to start?"

"Why don't you start with the last murder in Rotorua, and we'll take it from there."

He probably spoke for over an hour, occasionally prodded by me as I asked a pertinent question, but oh boy was Carl ready to talk! I don't think he was exactly boasting about his prowess, but he did his best to try to fill us in on any details we might want him to bring up.

"The last one was the bloke that got off with the rape of that bird. I met the bloke I was supposed to meet at the Palace, and he fingered the victim".

"So you're saying you were employed to deal with our murder victim? How did you meet the bloke in the pub? Did you have a signal or something?"

"No, nothing like that. I was supposed to be carrying a copy of the Hamilton newspaper from the previous day. As soon as I walked in, he came over to meet me by the door and told me which bloke needed to be dealt with and that was pretty much it, as far as he was concerned. He buggered off but it was a bit out of order sending a snooty bastard like that into that pub."

"So then what happened?"

"I had to wait around because he was drinking with his mates. His mates buggered off, probably around 9.30 and that let me get closer to him. I slipped a mickey into his beer and after that it was just a case of waiting for him to feel a bit under the weather."

"And then what happened?"

"Well, I followed him out and walked with him down to his car. He was literally all over the place, so I offered to give him a lift home. He was in no mood to care so he went to my car and then we went round the corner to the kill site."

His mention of the phrase 'kill site' made me a bit queasy but I tried to keep a straight face.

"And then what happened?"

"Well it was a bit of an anticlimax really. When I suggested we walk over to the bin he went like a lamb. It was almost too easy to get him over to the bin, do the deed and toss him in!"

"May I ask what does "Do the deed" mean exactly?"

"Oh yeah, I broke his neck, it was quick and clean. Within two minutes it was all over and done with. Hey, I'm sorry for picking out your back door. If I'd known, it was your place I might have picked somewhere different."

"And then what happened?"

"Oh yeah. You know when I get a job like that, I tend to get a bit excited, so I went to the first bird in the paper and gave her a bell. She was able to fit me in there and then, so I went to her place on Malfroy Road, wasn't it? She was great value."

"So then what happened?"

"Is that all you can say, Detective Sergeant? 'So then what happened'. Yeah, I had sex and then headed back to Hamilton. "

"So why the Shenanigans with the other working girl?"

"Well that was because of you, wasn't it? When I saw you walking to the dealership on Friday night and then you said you were a detective from Rotorua, I nearly crapped myself. I knew it was because of last week. Then you went on about your car having a sick motor I handed it off to one of the Saturday lads and got out of there. Then I thought I'd better get on down to Rotorua and tell the bird I'd shagged to keep her mouth shut. Then this other bird showed up, so I knew something was up. I might have been a bit rough with her. Sorry about that!"

"Look Carl. I know this was a bit rough on you, but I may have some other questions to ask you, OK?"

"Not a problem. Do you want to know about the other one I did in Rotorua now?"

He then told us how he had killed another person about two years ago in Rotorua. At her trial she'd been called the 'Angel of death', It turns out she'd been helping some of her patients cross the big gap. As the trial unfolded, it appeared that not all of her patients were that happy to cross over! It also seemed that a number of her patients had left her something in her will. I remembered the case. I think it belonged to the Boss. She'd gotten off on a technicality and there was insufficient evidence to convict her of most of the other cases, so she'd walked away, virtually scott free!

Carl did say that he had to inject her with something nasty and tell her what it was, so she knew she was going to die, and soon! When asked what he had used for the injection, Carl just laughed and said "I had some drain cleaner in the boot. We use it as a degreaser, so I used that. It wouldn't have made any difference to her. She was going to end up dead, no matter what. She didn't seem too pissed off, but we all do it differently."

The other two murders were committed in Auckland and South Auckland. When he spoke, in detail, of the cases I was immediately reminded of them. So, over the last three years Carl had committed four murders. I didn't know about the Boss, but I needed a break. All of this talk of casually killing someone, even if they probably deserved it, was making me angry!

The Boss did the formal part by saying the interview was suspended for ten minutes and then he took me outside to calm down.

When I had calmed down a little the Boss asked me to not forget about the murders and the assaults. As far as he was concerned a murder was no different than a beating or a case of shoplifting. It was all a crime statistic to be solved. I'd always taken a murder to be more personal, but it would help me be a bit more detached. While we were outside the Boss also asked me if I reckoned our guy was some sort of avenging angel who gave some justice out to those who gotten away with it with the Justice System? I said I'd ask if the opportunity came up. With that, we went back inside. Carl had been given a cup of tea by the guards, so he was quite refreshed and was ready to give us further details.

"So what do you lads want next? The beatings?"

I immediately went back to angry, so the Boss stepped in and said that would be a great place to start.

There was no stopping Carl when he was on a roll. He was quite happy to spill the beans on his other victims who had only suffered a beating, or as Carl put it, "A bloody good hiding."

"I think the first one was maybe two or two and a half years ago; it might have been three years ago. First, I must tell you that I got a baton from one of the provosts in our camp and I've kept it since. I've always used the baton because it's easily concealed and ready in a moment. For a beating I usually take a mate with me and split the fee. It's an easy five hundred notes each so my mate is usually up for it. Let me see, the first one was there in Rotorua. There was a wife beater who got a bit enthusiastic. I got the word, and I could do anything to him as long as he survived. We might have got a bit keen with him, but he survived and, as far as I know, it was never reported to the Cops. I think he lived up in Pleasant Heights, but I can't remember all the details now. It was my first job, so I was keen to make sure I did it right."

"The second one was in South Auckland, might have been in Glen Eden or Mount Eden. I don't remember, really. Again we gave him a good hiding, but we were a little more, what's the word, careful? We possibly went a bit far with the first one, so we were a bit more careful with this one. Again, I don't think this one was ever reported to the Cops, but at least it didn't make it into the papers."

"The third one, I have to scratch my head with this one. Oh yes, it was on Mount Roskill. Same thing, a bit of a beating and we left him behind a bus shelter. From memory the guy was showing himself to young girls. Evidently the Auckland mob reckoned that was worth a beating."

You mentioned the Auckland Mob. Who is that?

"Oh yeah, the Auckland Mob, I think they have their own fixer now. At least we haven't had any calls for the last year or so. Shame really. It was easy money, and we'd usually get a night in Auckland out of our money."

The Boss was suddenly taking an interest, so he asked the question. Can you explain about the Auckland Mob?

"Oh, yeah. Auckland has got two panels. Hamilton has got one. Tauranga and Rotorua have a panel each."

So what is a panel, what does it consist of?

"Maybe somewhere between a half dozen and ten blokes. I've never heard of a woman being involved. Yeah, between six and ten blokes. They might meet once a month more or less and they discuss anyone who's caught the eye of Johnny Law. I've heard that some never meet. It somehow protects their involvement. That's what I heard. Anyway, if this person got off Scott free, the 'Panel' might pay for a bloke like me to give them a visit. In extreme cases it might mean a visit from me, and then your bloke ends up in the rubbish skip like your lad did last week."

The Boss seemed a little taken aback but he hid it well.

"So there are a few other panels in the North Island?" I asked Carl.

"Well there's one in Napier. I hear there's one in Palmy and I'd be surprised if there wasn't one in Wellington! That's the ones I've heard of. There may be others in the South Island but if there are I haven't heard of them.

My mind was going at a speed of ten to the dozen as I tried to get my head around what Carl was saying.

The Boss was still pressing for further information.

"So who would be on one of these 'Panels'?"

Carl seemed remarkably affable, as if we were discussing which TV programmes, we watched last night.

"Well it wouldn't be the likes of you and me, would it. Nah, I'd guess it was blokes with a few bob behind them. I dunno, Rotary members? Freemasons? That type of bloke, but I'm guessing."

The Boss was trying to keep digging, "Would it be Just pakeha, er, white blokes?"

"Nah, the last job I did in Auckland, the contact was with a Pacific Island bloke. Nice guy he was. Quite apologetic about getting me up there to do their dirty business. The one before was the beating and that was a Māori bloke. Last week it was that white bloke, the posh one."

I intervened and asked how he got paid to do what he did.

"I usually get a parcel from the couriers. I got a grand for giving someone a good hiding and four grand for the full experience."

By now, the tape was getting full, and Carl was finally running out of steam, so we called it a day and said we'd be back the next day with it all typed up and ready to sign.

On the way back there were several moments when the Boss started a sentence and didn't finish it. I don't blame him. My head was in its own kind of whirl!

When we got back, we let the Sarge listen to the entire tape. When Carl got to the second murder the Sarge immediately jumped in with "I remember that!" He also said the same about the third and fourth murders.

When Carl spoke about the Rotorua beating, Sarge remembered having seen the wife beater in a poor way a few weeks after his court case and noticed he looked the worst for wear but never thought any more about it.

When Carl got round to talking about the "Panels" dotted around the big towns and cities in the North Island the Sarge had to sit down.

The Sarge rarely swore. This time he said something which was so unusual for the Sarge that even I switched on to how the Sarge was feeling.

The Sarge started with, "And it's been going on under our noses for years?"

"Never mind that, I have to get this over to the typist then we'll talk," said the Boss.

With that he buggered off over the road. I assumed he'd also have to report this to his Boss as well. This was a big development.

The Sarge and I sat for a minute. The Sarge seemed as blown away as I had been.

Fortunately the Sarge had a bit more experience in these types of things.

"So he got paid for coming down and working someone over on our patch. And he got four grand to kill some bugger. And then there's this 'Panel' who decide whether or not the bloke got enough justice from the court and then they reckon they have the final say."

Like me, the Sarge's mind was trying to clutch at everything to try and make some sense out of it.

"So who would be on this 'Panel'? Well there's Jeff Whiteley for a start. That reminds me I need to arrest that lad. Maybe I'll get him to come to the station with his lawyer. Arresting him will give the lawyer something to talk about and earn his money. Who else would be on the 'Panel', then?"

I'd already put my head to work on the way home and it could be literally any of the snobs in our town.

"I haven't a clue and I spent the last hour or so wondering about that. I wonder if any other organisations are involved in dishing out their own form of justice. What about the Maori elders? I reckon we have to rely on the Boss to give us a heads up on who might be on our list of targets."

The Sarge sort of agreed and then went off to phone Jeff Whiteley to ask him to come round to our office. When Jeff argued that his lawyer might be busy, the Sarge just stated, "If you're not here at four o'clock I'll send a squad car to your office to arrest you. It's your call" and then he hung up on Jeff. The Sarge could get a little bit aggro when he wanted to!

One thing we had to organise was a regular meeting with the Marae Elders. It was a once or twice yearly event held at our offices. There was a council of marae elders who got together and discussed anything important for the local Māori community. Once or twice a year we had a meeting at our place. It was a part of our outreach to the local community that the Big Boss insisted on. It was due to be held that afternoon at 1.30. Fortunately the Boss had grabbed the Bosses office when he moved over the road. It helped that the Boss could now comfortably accommodate the entire council of elders in his office. By grabbing every chair in the office we could get the assembled elders into the Bosses office. It was one of those meetings where the senior people had the comfiest chairs and the plebs got the less comfy ones. As a senior officer I had one of the comfy chairs and it was just a little amusing for me to watch as the elders tried to look inconspicuous when they selected which chair was sat on by who.

I have to be honest here and say I really don't care who your father was or his grandfather. So when the council of elders started to recite their lineage and how they had got to their position I was less than impressed. If anything, I may have turned off my attention span. It's a very slim possibility I may have snored or something that sounded like a snore. The Boss asked me to move as he brushed past me and got the sarge to sit in on the meeting. I quickly got the message that the sarge was there to mainly keep me awake and attentive. Once the formalities had been dealt with the meeting became a little more interesting for me. There was the usual chatter about kids no longer respecting the elders without a gentle cuff on the ear to remind them. My Boss mentioned the panel very subtly and a couple of the elders took it the wrong way. Before I could really gather what the fuss was about the meeting had taken on a very much 'them and us' mentality. I think that somehow in the general business being explained, the issue of the panel had been taken to be a Māori thing and was being held as Māori violence inherent in their system. This was totally not what the boss was trying to say but a couple of the hotheads decided to take it that way and the meeting descended into chaos.

We were best not adding fuel to the fire but the elders were now disappointed in our attitude. This completely ignored the fact that the Boss had not explained it that way at all. The meeting ended sooner than the usual hour or so of discussion and the Elders all trooped out of the room. The Boss reckoned it would be within a half hour and the Big Boss would be getting a call to complain about the DI. He wasn't too bothered as he had other things to worry about.

Withing a half hour, the Boss was called over to the Big Bosses office and asked to explain. My Boss tried to defer the matter by saying we had a suspect in the 'panel'. That allowed the Big Boss to say he wanted to be in at the collars of this group.

By now the Boss had returned from over the road. He'd had a meeting with the big Boss and he wanted to be in on our meetings. However my Boss had done a number on him by saying that he already knew most of the people in town with his Rotary connections and his lodge connections etc, so it might be better if we kept it at CIB level only and only invited the Boss in if we had a person of interest that the big Boss might be able to help with. The Big Boss, the ACI, had reluctantly agreed to it. So at least we weren't going to have the ACI interfering with our collars!

The Boss agreed to sit in on the interview/ arrest of Jeff Whitely and that would be our next job. As it was already after three, the Boss arranged to have a squad car available if Jeff was a no show.

At a few minutes before four o'clock Jeff and his lawyer walked in. Jeff was complaining about how this was affecting his business dealings, so the Boss and I took Jeff and his lawyer into the interview room.

The Boss was not really in a mood to be trifled with, so he got straight down to the nitty gritty. He laid out what Carl had said this morning and the lawyer answered most of the questions with 'no comment'. That was enough for the Boss.

He formally charged Jeff Whiteley with conspiracy to commit murder in the first degree. He carried on by reading him his rights despite the lawyer's protest. Jeff looked stunned! His face was ashen when the Boss asked him if he understood his rights and it was only when the lawyer nudged him that he gave a sign and then, at the Boss's suggestion he verbally acknowledged what the Boss had said to him. The Boss then offered Jeff a deal about turning King's evidence and left Jeff and his solicitor alone in the interview room to discuss what had been spoken about.

When the Boss and I walked outside of the room, the Boss said "Well, that went better than I expected. He knows we have him bang to rights and his lawyer is on to it as well. Maybe we'll get a deal out of him."

My concern was the fact that with him being a Rotary member we'd have a hard time finding a local Judge who would not recuse themselves from the case because they knew him from Rotary or the Masons or whatever.

The Boss hadn't thought of that, so he got on the phone to his mate at the Taupo Copshop and arranged to have one of their Judges in the Rotorua Court the next morning. I tell you, when the Boss is in the right mood, nothing will stand in his way.

By that time we were asked to go back into the interview room with Jeff and his lawyer. Note, we were asked to go back into the interview room. We weren't summoned. By that we knew that Jeff knew he was in deep trouble.

The lawyer started his prepared response, "Might I ask, Detective Inspector, when you earlier intimated that a deal may be achievable are you able to be a little more specific."

The Boss had the feeling we may be onto a winner here. Heck, even I could see Jeff was beaten.

Conspiracy to commit murder in the first degree is classed in New Zealand courts as if the offender actually committed the murder, which carried a range of 15 years to life. The Boss said we had not had time to see if Jeff was guilty of conspiracy for the other crimes. That would add, possibly considerably, to Jeff's time inside. Possibly Jeff could be looking in a worst case scenario at anything up to twenty years of Porridge.

Again we were asked to step outside.

We couldn't hear them talking and the interview room had no adjoining room, so we waited in the CIB room until we were invited in again.

It was probably at least after 5.00pm when we were asked back into the interview room.

We waited for the lawyer to speak first.

"My client is more than willing to assist the Police with their enquiries on this matter if we can receive some regard for the fact that he has helped you with those enquiries."

The Boss was straight onto it, "Let's talk about time inside. He's looking at 15 years or so. Any deal I can offer has to be run by the CP, obviously, but let's talk about time inside. What are you hoping for?"

The lawyer was straight back with, "A maximum of five years and he will tell you of at least two people, he believes may also be involved with this incident."

The Boss replied with, "He's dreaming if he wants to be out in five. Let's say ten years and I'll take it to the CP."

The lawyer was up for the argument," Let's say eight years and you will not mention my client's name to the CP at this stage."

The Boss replied, with a straight face, "Eight years and I won't mention your client's name to the CP. That's it. Take it or leave it. We can wait outside while you talk."

At that the Boss stood up but the lawyer said, "We'll take that! Please put that to the Crown Prosecutor. Now what will happen to my client hereafter."

The Boss explained that the client would be put in the holding cells across the road at the new Police station. From there he would appear in front of a judge in the morning. He also explained that a judge was driving up from Taupo to oversee this case. "It's up to that Judge whether or not he will release Jeff on bail, but we will, as a matter of course ask for no bail as it is a crime of a serious nature."

The lawyer completely understood. Jeff was another matter. He was almost in tears.

We got up and left the lawyer and Jeff talking. I have to say that the Boss and I did a high-five when we got out of the door. Now the Boss had to go and see the Crown Prosecutor and do another deal with him. Fortunately the Boss was persuasive, or the CP was in a good mood, so he readily agreed to maximum 8 year term.

By the time that the Boss returned, the lawyer had left, and Jeff was now in the shiny new holding cells across the road.

The Boss emailed the lawyer and then went over to see Jeff and tell him that his negotiations with the CP had been successful. Jeff was a little surprised the Boss did not want to interview him immediately. He did remind Jeff that he should put in his apologies for that night's Rotary meeting!

While he was over at the new Copshop the Boss checked that his typing was ready for Carl Jeffries to sign. It was ready so he brought it back ready to go to Waikeria the next morning.

I indicated that tomorrow might be a problem if one of us had to go to Waikeria and one of us was supposed to be opposing bail for Jeff in the Rotorua high court.

The Boss suggested that I go over to Waikeria and get Carl to sign his confession and that he would appear in the High Court to oppose Jeff's bail. With that and six o'clock approaching we all headed off home.

Wednesday

I was in as usual fairly early in the morning but was still beaten in by the Sarge. Once we had our coffee in hand we set about the business of the day. With it being a Wednesday morning we were fairly light on incidents reported that may have wanted CIB input. The 'security men' visiting the homeless had been up to their usual tricks and we had, perhaps, five of them in the cells. We left the two DCs to look after that side of things. Then we had a thank you to the two new plods who I had worked with for the first week or so. They would be heading back to the squad room over the road and would be rostered for street patrols and the like. I reckoned that either of them would make a reasonable DC if they ever got the chance and I managed to get that written in their report cards.

I went over to Waikeria, and the Boss was due to go the High court and oppose Jeff's bail.

Well I was successful! I got Carl to sign his statement with no problems. I must admit that I had taken the Sarge's advice to remain calm and I got a little more out of Carl during my time at Waikeria. There was nothing major in what we chatted about, but I did learn about his time in the army. He was something of a wild child in the army. He didn't like taking orders, so he spent a bit of time in the clink. He did mention that he's learned a lot in the army about how to kill people. He went into some detail, but I was not as attentive as I might have been. We had what we wanted.

The Boss had a less than successful day in court. He was up against a sharp QC who emphasised his client's sterling work in the community etc. The long and the short of it was that Jeff Whitely had to give up his passport and report once a day to the main copshop. As his trial would be a minimum of three months away, it was deemed unfair to have him inside for that amount of time.

While the Boss may have been fuming at this development, he was now focused on how he could get Jeff to give up his associates. The Boss and the Sarge and I discussed the whole issue over our lunch.

The Sarge went first, "He's probably initially been approached by his Rotary mates. Get him to talk about his mates and we might find out a bit more."

The Boss reckoned he knew all of Jeff's Rotary mates and he couldn't imagine any of Jeff's mates being a part of this 'Panel'.

I was going to wait until we had Jeff in our interview room. He knew he had to give up at least two of the 'Panel' to get his plea for reduced jail time.

The Boss reckoned we should start as we meant to go on and tell Jeff that we expected him into our interview room, without or without his brief, this afternoon.

As expected, we went with the Boss's idea. That's why he's the Boss!

The Sarge rang him, and Jeff was all happy to be in our interview room by 3.pm.

Jeff was a little cautious when we sat down in our interview room. He wanted to go over the details of how he could get a sentence reduction. Fortunately, the Sarge knew him socially and was able to convince him that our deal was above board.

The only thing that Jeff really knew was that two other Rotary members had approached him in a semi casual conversation and the topic of conversation was along the lines of 'have you had a call yet?" and "how did you vote?'

To my mind Jeff's claim to be helping us with our enquiries seemed a little bit thin but the Sarge was taking the lead in this conversation, so I just went along with it. It occurred to me that I was being fairly passive in letting the Sarge take the lead, but I was taking notes and I did have the odd question to chip in.

Eventually we got two names out of Jeff. One name was Terence Hohepa and the other was Craig Mansell.

Terence Hohepa was a barrister in town who regularly went along to the Court hearing sessions. Arriving around 9.30 he would let it be known he was available as a legal aid brief. He made good money out of appearing for pretrial hearings based on the previous night's activity by the Police. He would usually end up with a couple of cases of drunk and disorderly or a case of Grievous Bodily Harm. By representing the felons at their hearing for bail he would often get kept on as a retainer for the full hearing. As I said, he made a quite reasonable living out of his barrister-ship.

The other guy, Craig Mansell, was a completely different kettle of fish. Craig was a prim and proper old school kind of guy. Never married, he was an architect who always seemed to want to be accepted. Always ready to give out to charity, he was a long-time member of Rotary. If there was a wall full of sponsorship bricks, you'd always find Craig's name on the wall. A nice enough sort of guy but just a little bit odd. It didn't really surprise me when his name came up.

Neither Terence nor Craig were available in the morning so I arranged for Terence to come in after lunch the next day. He was usually available in the afternoon. The Boss wanted to 'sit in' on the interview through the glass one way mirror in the interview rooms so we had the Interview over the road at the new interview rooms so the Boss could overhear and see what was going on.

Chapter 8

T**hursday**

As I did not have that much to do, I went and visited one of my confidential informants. It was unusual for me to visit in the morning but I was quite excited to be making such good progress on a case, so I went along to see Tiffany. Yeah, she had nothing to add to my case, but we managed to pass the time. She also mentioned that she had heard about one of the 'girls' getting worked over. I told her it had been taken care of and we already had the guy inside. She somehow felt a little safer knowing that we had already dealt with the case.

My Boss didn't want to be one of the interviewing detectives because he was also a Rotary member, so he had me and the Sarge present when Terrence arrived to be interviewed. He figured it might be a little more conducive to getting the truth out of the suspect.

Once we had sat down comfortably, I opened the chat with the following.

"So, Terence, we're interested in a phone call you had last Monday evening. Would you care to relay what the call was about."

I'd had word from Jeff that he had received a call on Monday evening. I assumed that Terence would have received his phone call on the same night.

Terence thought about his response for a second or two." Well I was told it was confidential and it was on that basis that I agreed to take part in the call. I seldom get a call after hours so I can remember this chat."

It was like pulling teeth!

So I asked again to phrase it a little differently this time, "So who was the call from?"

Terence replied, "Well I assume that you know all about this, though why it should be of concern to the constabulary is a mystery. Yes, my call was from John Shorter."

I carefully, but casually wrote the name down. If this was what it would take to find out who the members of the 'Panel' were, I was prepared to go as slowly as I needed to.

"And is this John Shorter a member of the 'Panel', also?"

Terence chuckled, "In Rotary we call it a member of the board of directors."

I tried a different tack, "May I ask what the call was concerning?"

"Again, I would ask your indulgence and explain that this is specifically regarded as a matter of confidence by all in this room, and anyone who may be listening."

Once again, I believed I was indulging him by agreeing to any fantasy that our discussion would be confidential for long, given the seriousness our charges presented. It was also useful to know that Terence was aware that someone may be listening to his conversation, on the other side of the one-way mirror.

I nodded to Terence indicating confidentiality.

Terence continued, seemingly reluctantly, "John Shorter is a member of the Rotary board of directors and is charged with responsibility for the Service and Outreach committee. He contacted me to say that TVNZ were considering reviving the 'Top Town show'. In previous years the local Kiwanis Club has handled the organisation of such an event. John had been approached by the producers of the show to consider whether Rotary might be willing to take it on. Evidently it is acknowledged as a huge fundraiser. John was sounding me out as to whether we would consider taking it on. I believe he also spoke to several other members of the Service and Outreach committee. I'm afraid no decision has yet been reached as to whether the project will get the green light."

I tried not to appear as stupid as I felt. I'm sure the Sarge was also feeling a little let down.

"So did you get any calls for anyone who is not a member of your Rotary Club?" Immediately I knew I had given him another easy out.

Terence was actually enjoying this repartee, it seemed he was enjoying it a damn sight more than I was! "Well on the Wednesday night, or it may indeed have been the Thursday night, I did get a call from a person purporting to be from my bank, but it seemed so preposterous I dismissed the caller and actually hung up on him."

"Terence, I may have got off on the wrong tack. You do realise we are here to discuss any possible involvement with the 'Panel", that you may have?" It was probably one of the more stupid things I have said. You never give the interviewee any indication of what you are looking for. It gives them the element of denial.

He responded with, "Oh, this is that thing that Whiteley was booked for. Please continue."

I replied with, "Terence, you had a conversation with Jeff Whiteley on your club night. You asked him had he had a phone call?"

"Oh, yes, now I see where you are coming from. Yes, I asked him if he had received a phone call from John Shorter, about the Top Town thing, the programme."

"Yet you also asked him which way he had voted?"

"Yes, I was obviously asking him how he had voted for our club taking on the programme, the Top Town thing? Oh. You think that I was involved with this 'Panel' thing. Good heavens no!"

I knew I was well beaten. This guy was used to thinking on his feet in the courtroom. The Sarge stepped in and tried to save the situation.

"May I ask, Terence, what is your actual involvement with the 'Panel'?"

For some reason, his reply really made me angry! "This is quite a situation for me. I already know your Boss and your Chief Inspector...

I couldn't help interrupting, "You mean our *Acting* Chief Inspector!"

Seemingly without missing a beat, Terrence replied, "Well, he has a long history with the Police force, and he has a long and proud history with his marae which is the main marae for this area. It's a formality, surely."

I was about to interrupt again when the Sarge touched my arm and overrode me, "Apologies, Mr. Hohepa, you were saying?"

Our client then looked the Sarge squarely in the eyes and said, "Firstly, I get asked questions by a Detective Sergeant. Now I am asked questions by a desk sergeant. I'm really going down the chain of command. You are both aware that I am a personal friend of your immediate superior and also the Area Commander. I wonder who will be next to enquire about my health. A meter maid perhaps?"

The Sarge was too cool to rise to the bait, but I knew he was well annoyed! So he repeated the question.

Although he looked at me, his reply was to the Sergeant. "Let's stop dancing around, shall we? Let me ask you two, what evidence do you have that I have absolutely any involvement with this group or 'Panel'. If I may paraphrase the situation, I would suggest that you put up or shut up!"

With this now developing into a standoff, I asked the Sarge to step outside.

Outside, in the hallway we were met by the Boss.

The Boss was understandably annoyed, but with the two of us!

"He's got you two on a string and he knows it! You have nothing to prove he's anything to do with the 'Panel' other than the hearsay of Jeff Whiteley. Let him go and we'll get the next bloke in as soon as we can." With that he turned away and walked back to our offices.

Sarge and I went back into the interview room where Terence awaited us.

Both the Sarge and I tried a few other ways of approaching the situation but with each question we were met with "Prove it!"

After a further ten minutes we let him go and thanked him for his time. He was smirking when he left. He knew he had us beaten but the interesting thing was how quickly he went on the offensive..

We walked over to the temporary offices, both knowing we were going to hear more from the Boss about this opportunity we had squandered.

The two DCs were out of the office so it was just me, the Sarge and the Boss.

The Boss let fly, "You were both a right pair of amateurs in there and that sleazebag ran rings around you both! Yes, I know you are limited to what you can say to a suspect but there are ways of asking questions that you pair never even tried!"

The Sarge looked more than a little annoyed. For me I was always trying to improve my interview technique, so I asked him, "Okay, Boss, you just said that we were tied down as to what we can ask. How would you have handled it?"

The Boss looked a little annoyed, but he did give us a few clues. "Well, for a start be more assumptive with your questions. Instead of saying where you were on the night of, you could try saying "Okay, we know that you were at such and such a place, did you use the murder weapon or did your mate use it, and then shut the hell up. The next one who speaks is the loser!"

Before the Sarge could say anything, I asked how we would handle that in the confession.

The Boss looked up at the ceiling before his reply. I think he was trying to not say that we were stupid, but he changed his mind and said, "When the bloke signs his confession it's never a word for word of what they said, it's, at best, a summary of what was said. So you incorporate what was said and unless they object, they will sign the thing. Instead of asking did you pull the shooter out, you ask if it were you carrying the gun when you entered the shop. Look, you two have another interview this afternoon with Craig Mansell. He should be easy to roll over but could you two please try out a new questioning technique."

At 4 pm Craig Mansell presented himself at the new Copshop and we conducted him into the interview room. The Sarge and I were doing the interview and the Boss was behind the one-way mirror viewing the proceedings. I have to say that I was even more nervous knowing that the Boss was now listening for every word I said.

I introduced myself and the Sarge and we got down to business.

I opened with the fact that Craig and Jeff Whiteley had a conversation at their previous Rotary meeting. I could see Craig's face drop as I started speaking about Jeff Whiteley. Somehow that brightened my day, but I was careful not to let it show.

I continued, "Craig, I know you spoke about the subject of the recent murder victim. May I ask which of you first brought up the name of the murder victim."

Craig replied, "Neither of us did. His name wasn't mentioned as far as I can recollect." That was already a huge improvement from the conversation I had with Terence Hohepa. I reckon the Boss might be onto something with this way of interviewing a suspect.

"But you both were aware of who you were discussing?"

"Yes, obviously, but you need to be aware that I only wanted the bugger to get given a beating. It wasn't right what he did to that young girl!"

"Craig, may I ask who gave you a phone call to discuss the fate of the victim?"

'I don't know. It's always the same bloke but he has a thing on the phone that distorts his voice. I don't know what they call it."

"So am I right in assuming you got the call on the Monday evening?"

"Yes."

"Did this person call from a cell phone or was it from a land line?"

"It was always from a landline, why would that matter? And it was always a bloke that called and I'm pretty sure it was always the same bloke."

"How did he start the conversation? Did he give you some information about the offender?"

Craig was in his element now. He did like to be agreeable with people, even if he didn't realise it, he was digging himself into a deeper hole.

"Well he asked me if I had heard of this bloke. And when I said I had, he gave me a bit of a rundown on this bloke's record and the latest crime he's gotten off with. He asked whether I reckoned this bloke had been fairly judged and when I said he'd gotten away with it, this bloke asked me what I reckoned should happen to this bloke. I reckoned a good beating would do, providing the bloke knew why he was getting a good hiding."

"Then what happened, Craig."

"Well that was about it. He thanked me for my continued service to the community and after that, I don't know, he probably just hung up."

In summary, Craig had just effectively confessed to being a part of the 'Panel' so I told him we would have to charge him with the offense of conspiring to commit murder in the first degree. To say he was less than happy would be an understatement. His reply that he was only saying that the bloke should have a beating was not a defense as far as we were concerned. We did not push him to tell us about any other murders or anything else.

I offered him the plea deal that if he would give us the names of his co-conspirators, we could make his sentence more lenient, but it fell on deaf ears. He didn't really know who his 'upline' was and we already had the name of Jeff Whiteley and his confession in the bag.

I gave the Craig the opportunity to sit and think about it for a moment while we stepped outside and consulted with the Boss.

The Boss was obviously thrilled that we had another confession when we heard a banging on the mirror, so we returned to the interview room and Craig was busy trying to look through the one-way glass when we returned to the room.

He turned round as we entered, 'Yes, I've got a name for you buggers to work with! It's Johnny, whatever his name is. He's a new member. His name is Johnny something or other. It's er...er.. Got it! Johnny Warburton. The new bloke. He's got a garage up in View Road. Not in View Road. It's the one off of it. Riri Street. That's it. He thought everybody was in this 'Panel' thing when you became a member of Rotary. I told him he'd better not spread that around. But you're right, I did have a word with him about the 'Panel' and he did say he'd been given a phone call about this last bloke, the one you found in your rubbish skip. That's got to be worth a lighter time inside, hasn't it?"

I agreed that it was indeed a consideration and that we would mention it to the Crown Prosecutor when we told him all of the facts of the case.

With nothing further to act upon we charged Craig with conspiracy and he also noted that we hadn't mentioned anything about the new bloke he's dobbed in. So we got the typist to type up a charge sheet and mentioned that Craig had been eager to make a plea deal. Craig seemed happy enough. We told him he would spend the night in the cells, but we'd release him on bail the next day with the same reporting conditions as Jeff Whiteley. We didn't go through the rigmarole of a proper hearing. We all knew that Craig would be released so we just went with it.

With that we escorted Craig down to the cells and returned to our hideaway across the road.

The Boss was delighted, not only with our advancement of the case but also with our taking a more flexible approach when interviewing Suspects.

With that, it was after five o'clock, so we called it a day and went home. All in all, a good days work!

Friday

We were in bright and early for the next day and ready to call in our next witness/suspect. The two DC's were busy processing the charge sheets for the Black Power lads we had pulled in for the supply of drugs etc. The Sarge reported that a body had been found in the scrub past the Sudima Hotel. It had been discovered by a couple of cyclists who had wandered off the path. The Boss took this on and I continued with my paperwork for the murder case. Evidently the body was just that of a homeless guy who did not want to be subject to the rules of living in a motel etc. The Boss got the fingerprint lads to go and look around and the pathologist, Mike, was called in. Once Mike got the body back to the morgue he was able to quickly establish that the guy was a drunk who had literally overdone it with the drink. Part of me felt a little sorry for this guy but a part of me was sort of pleased he had done himself in and he had not been the victim of some of the street kids you hear about.

It might have been around 9.30 when we got a call that Carl Jeffries had had another attempt made on his life. Carl was in surgery at the Waikato Hospital. As was his assailant. It appeared that Carl had gotten off better than the assailant. The Boss made a phone call and asked Johnny Warburton to put back his time to come and see us until this afternoon. Johnny Warburton did ask about our meeting, but the Boss fobbed him off by saying we had to shoot over to Hamilton to see a man about a case in Hamilton.

The Boss and I headed over to the Waikato Hospital to see how Carl was. On the way over the Boss let me in on a few trade secrets about interviewing suspects. He probably felt safer while he was in his car. I had always gone by the book when I interviewed suspects and witnesses. And the Boss let me know that it was ok to occasionally bend the rules. He said he would usually back me up with a witness or suspect interview 'unless I had been stupid' I certainly got the feeling that I was now a bit more in with the Boss.

When we arrived at Waikato Hospital we were shown into Carl's own room. There was a guard outside and we had to show our Police ID to get in. The Boss reckoned it was about time the locals started to get a bit more serious with this case.

Inside Carl was quite cheerful, "I was taking a shower and this bloke was getting a bit too close. When you're stark naked and a bloke comes a bit too close, you get a bit wary. Maybe I've been in the army too long, but I was already a bit iffy and then the bastard pulled a shiv on me. He got me in the lower back, but I was always ready for him. He barely scraped my skin when I was already half turned and I may have put the knife back in his own gut, I may have 'inadvertently' pulled on the knife when it was in. It's entirely possible that he may have come off a bit worse than I did."

The Boss asked me to go and find out the damage to Carl's assailant. When I did find out, it wasn't pretty. Evidently Carl had stuck the shiv in and then done a 'Hari Kiri" maneuver. If you don't know what that means, look it up for yourself. Carl was a killing machine, and he was very versatile!

The assailant had received surgery and was now in intensive care, and likely to be in there for a few days. Survival was not necessarily guaranteed but the hospital staff were 'reasonably optimistic'.

When I returned to Carl's room he was grinning, "How is the poor sod? I really do hope he does get better."

I reported to the Boss about the assailant's condition. He wasn't too surprised. Carl was a very compact fighter, and anyone would need to be on their toes if they wanted to take Carl on. Carl had been asking the Boss when his trial would be. He figured the attempts on his life would probably go down when he was found guilty. And Carl was right. There was a school of thought, that we had discussed in our office, was whether we would have a case if something happened to Carl.

I was confident that having Carl in Court would be a massive boost to our cause, but it wouldn't be the end of the world if Carl wasn't available.

The Boss wondered whether we would still have a case that the CP would want to take forward, without Carl being there.

We discussed, with Carl, the possibility of putting Carl in the area reserved for 'on remand' people. Carl didn't want a bar of that talk. He thought he would be better off in the general population area of the prison. That way he could buddy up to a mate that would keep an eye out for him while he slept. I hadn't thought that being inside a prison was a place where you could get yourself sorted while on remand. But Carl was aware of the opportunities available inside and how to get the most out of the situation. I assumed it was because Carl had spent a bit of time in the Army, locked up, that he was so conversant with the system.

We also spoke with Carl about our three suspects. Well, two suspects and a strong hunch. Carl had never heard of Jeff Whiteley, Carl Mansell and Johnny Warburton. When we reminded Carl that he had met Jeff Whiteley, he remembered that he was the 'Posh bloke from the Pub'.

We left Carl alone with his guard and returned to Rotorua.

The Boss was a little quieter on the way back and it didn't faze me too much as I had a few thoughts going on in my head, mainly about how structured life could be inside the Nick if you knew how to rig the system.

When we got back, the Sarge wanted to know how we had fared at the Waikato Hospital. The Boss had had a call from the ACI wanting to know why the Boss had stood him up at their weekly meeting. The

Boss wandered over to see the big Boss while I filled in the Sarge on Carl's latest adventures.

The Sarge wasn't surprised that another attempt had been made on Carl's life. He also wasn't surprised that Carl had done more damage to the assailant than he had received in the attack. The Sarge had a fairly negative view of those people who wanted the youth of today sent to 'Boot camps.' All we would end up with was a bunch of young thugs that now knew how to kill people on the taxpayer's dollar. He did have a point!

At 2.00 we had Johnny Warburton booked in for an interview, so we sat down and had our lunch. For a real change we discussed not the latest case, but Sarge's idea that he might consider getting a boat. Yes, he had talked about it with Jeff Whiteley, but it was more of a ruse to get him into the Station. The Sarge was actually considering a boat might be a decent way to get him and the Missus away for the weekend. And I if behaved myself I might get the odd invite for an evening's fishing.

The Boss interrupted our chat by announcing that the ACI wanted to eavesdrop on our interview with the latest suspect. The Boss did say I would have to behave myself in the interview room and make sure everything was by the book. I agreed to behave myself and a little before two we wandered over the road for the interview.

On the dot of two Johhny Warburton walked in to the new Copshop with his lawyer.

We took them down to the Interview room and set our case out.

A lot of what we said was supposition, and the lawyer was well versed in telling his client to shut up or whether he could answer our questions. I don't know how we got there but we eventually found ourselves making headway and the suspect began giving us more than we expected. Eventually, the lawyer asked for time alone with his client, so Sarge and I headed out of the room and the Boss and the ACI joined us in the corridor.

The Boss was congratulating us on our masterly way of interrogation. This confused me as I was only doing what I had done with our first suspect yesterday. The ACI was not quite moaning about our performance as we had just about a confession sewn up. He was bemoaning the fact that we hadn't gathered any new names to the list. The Boss carried on over the ACI which gave us a respite from his moaning and then we heard a knock on the Interview room door which was our signal to go back in.

The lawyer was doing the speaking, "If my client was to make any admission to this crime it would be on the strictest understanding that he was in no way a party to any other crimes that this group may or may not have carried out before he joined the Rotary club. It must also be taken into account that if my client had allegedly had a conversation with a person or persons unknown that he would have only given his permission for a physical assault to have occurred and in no way would my client wished to have been a party to a murder?"

I couldn't believe my ears. This lawyer and his client were rolling over for being a part of the 'Panel'.

I composed myself. At the side of me I could sense the Sarge was grinning from ear to ear, but just on the inside.

As best as I could reply to this lawyer-speak, I replied, "Unfortunately the case did resolve itself with a murder of the first degree, so that is what your client would be charged with. If your client wishes to throw himself at the mercy of the court, that would be his choice. However, I can allow that if the client wishes to plead guilty to the murder, or the conspiracy thereof, I can reveal we already have a number of people who have been charged with the same offence and have accepted a reduced term for co-operating with the police in the further investigation of this murder. Would you like a little further time with your client to discuss the matter further?"

Obviously, the lawyer asked for a little more time and the Sarge, and I left the interview room. Outside in the corridor the Boss and the ACI were waiting for us.

The ACI was the first to speak. I thought we would be in for a little praise, but the ACI had a different idea. "If that bloke has just joined the Rotary club, then he probably won't know any other names! So why did you offer him a plea deal?"

Fortunately, the Boss spoke up, "Well if he gives us any names, we're on a winner. If he doesn't give us any names, then he will have to take his chance in court."

The ACI was not convinced but he didn't say anything more. He walked off, to his office, I assume, muttering something about modern policing or something to that end. It was fairly obvious to everyone present that the ACI would be happier if I wasn't a member of his staff.

The Boss just said," Don't worry about him. He always has his knickers in a knot when it comes to the CIB. I think you both did well given the restraints that the big Boss was watching you do everything by the book. Listen it seems like the lawyer is having a bit of a word in there. Do you fancy a cup of tea? Maybe we'll take a look at the posh new facilities?"

We wandered upstairs into the new canteen. He was right, it was a posh place! They had three girls and a guy operating behind the counter and we received our cups of tea in fairly posh cups and saucers.

We'd barely sat down when we got the word that the lawyer was ready to speak to us. The Boss decided we would have our tea and go down when we were ready to go downstairs.

I was actually seeing a little bit of the Boss that I hadn't really seen before. He was quite tactical in his thinking. If we had scurried down when the lawyer summoned us it would have shown that we were running to the lawyer and his client. If we waited until we were ready, it somehow seemed to shift the power back onto our side. I liked it and committed it to memory as a handy thing to be aware of.

It was probably ten minutes later when the Sarge and I walked back into the interview room. Obviously, the Boss was on the other side of the one-way mirror. The Boss had impressed on me that the first person to speak loses power, so I kept my mouth shut. Fortunately, for us, the ACI was no longer listening to every word we might have said.

It might only have been perhaps ten seconds, but it seemed like an eternity and then the lawyer spoke on behalf of his client.

"My client is willing to accept that he was consulted on the fate of the victim but will only plead guilty on the assumption that he is charged with the lesser offence of conspiracy to commit assault. As he has only recently become a member of this club, he is unable to add any further names to your ongoing investigations, but he is willing to co-operate with any further enquiries that you may pursue on the understanding that the court will be made aware of his willingness to co-operate with the Police."

I looked at the Sarge and he nodded for me to continue. In reply I explained that we could frame the charge as conspiracy to assault but as the victim had indeed died because of the attack, it was over to the court to determine whether his client was a conspirator to assault or a conspirator to murder. I also indicated that we would make the court aware of the accused's willingness to co-operate with the Police.

With that we offered to leave the lawyer to consult with his client but after a shake of the head by the accused, the lawyer agreed to allow us to charge his client.

I was pleased now that we had three of the 'Panel' on the hook. That, along with Carl Jeffries at Waikeria, it gave us a group of four, which we could chalk up as a win. As far as getting anybody else, I figured we might be pushing our luck, but that wouldn't stop me trying!

We also were fairly certain that Terence Hohepa was a member of the 'Panel', but I knew we would have a really hard job of getting him to admit anything. Our issue was that he was so used to dealing with the

Police on a day-to-day basis, with his job, that he could wangle his way out of most things we could come up with against him.

At five-ish I went home and busied myself cooking my tea. I sat and watched the box for an hour or so and then had an early night.

<u>Monday</u>

On the Monday I awoke to a phone call from the Boss. It seems he had to go back over to Hamilton. Although the case was only set down for one day there was some bird from the 'Youth Justice Department' who had spent the better part of two hours going on about how these poor children needed some guidance and improvement in their life. For me and the Boss, being sufficiently organised to steal a car and then ram it into the front of a dairy, grab a swag of cigarettes and then try to leg it away in another motor, which was also stolen, smacked that these kids were fairly well organised and perhaps needed something more than a pat on the back and tissue if they were a little bit upset. But I digress. The Boss was headed back to Hamilton, and I had to keep myself occupied for the day. Oh, and the Boss told me about the profit margins in stolen smokes. It seems that smokes were selling for an average of forty dollars a packet in Hamilton. Getting twenty bucks for a pack of smokes, even if they were a bit dodgy, was way too easy for these lads. Two hundred dollars for a carton was the going rate in Hamilton and if these lads grabbed say ten cartons that was good for a couple of grand. That alone was bad enough but when you factored in, they might be stealing twenty or thirty grands worth of motors to carry out these ram raids, you can quickly see how it soon adds up to a major crime.

It was a lovely and sunny morning as I wandered into the Station and the Sarge reminded me that it was my turn to go and get the coffees. Walking over to the Library café I was pleased that I was going to see Annie at the café. She was always pleasant to chat to and she asked me what I was working on, now that the body in the rubbish skip was over and done with. I told her that solving the crime was the easy part of the job. Doing all the paperwork was always the hardest part of the job. She laughed and said that was why she was only a barista. No paperwork doing that job.

On returning to the temporary Cop shop, as usual I went to the back door and the rubbish skip was no longer there. On mentioning this to the Sarge he said he'd spoken to the builders, and they were virtually finished with their job next door. Within a week the new tenants would be in. To me it sounded less than pleasant. For the last three years, since the new Cop Shop opened, we had enjoyed relatively easy parking. Now we would be fighting for space like we had been in the previous days when all of the Cops were over in the temporary building. Ah, I'd deal with that later in the week!

Chapter 9

Over our coffee, the Sarge and the two DCs were chatting about our week ahead. The two DCs had to report to the Crown Prosecutor on Wednesday to hand over their case work, in order for the CP to prepare his case. The Sarge had lost out on a boat on Trade me. He'd been following it all along and he'd bid up to $17,500 because it was a good machine. Then he'd dithered about going up to $18,000 and he had lost out on it while he was dithering. I mentioned the Boss having to be over in Hamilton another day and I also mentioned the price of dodgy fags in Hamilton going for $20 a packet. It was only then I remembered that Dave Powell was a smoker. Yes, he did the mouth spray and stuff but he was known to shoot out the back of our office when the pressure was on, to have a smoke. Surprisingly the Sarge also spoke. He reckoned his missus would be up for a bit of that. She only has the odd one now and again but when she comes home from her Line Dancing, he can smell it on her.

That surprised me. I didn't know that Huia smoked. Well, you can still be surprised by people you know. The Sarge also spotted that Dave Powell was interested in the dodgy smokes until the Sarge mentioned in passing that current coppers and dodgy smokes were a poor mix.

Halfway through the previous Sunday I'd finally had the thought that had been eluding me for the past few days. For the motels and hotels, we'd been going after the foot soldiers, the Face-to-face drug suppliers. Why were we not going after the leaders? I raised that point while we were all having our coffee.

Dave Besant said it was on the Boss's recommendations. The Squad cars and the two DCs would go after the foot soldiers and the Boss would be having a word with everyone once they were in the cells. I'd spoken to the Boss, and he'd said that the Black Power mob were seeing it as something of a rite of passage doing a little bit of time. I remembered that conversation. I reckoned I might have a go at Jacko. He was nominally in charge of the 'Security men' and it might be worth having a conversation. I had nothing else to do!

After our coffee I rang this 'Jacko'. He didn't get in until 10 am or at least the office wasn't attended until then. I declined to leave a message and decided to ring back after 10 o'clock.

At about 10.30 I rang again and got through to Jacko. He said he was always pleased to help the police with their enquiries so he would not mind seeing me but could he possibly do it that afternoon around 2pm. Not a problem for me so I agreed. It's just as well because the Sarge reminded me that with the Boss in Hamilton, someone had better deal with the cases that were still mounting up from the weekend. I allocated the cases between myself and the two DCs

I was still in the office when I got a call from the Boss. He'd had his say in court in Hamilton and would be back in our office by midafternoon.

I left the office and went to my first case - a domestic assault in Springfield. So I went up to Nikau St. There was already a Squad car in attendance when I arrived. By the time I got there the hubby had been arrested and it was down to me to convince the wife that she should press charges. I have to say that these cases are often a waste of our time as the injured party has to want to press charges against the other party. Nine times out of ten it never happens, and this was one of those times. Yes, the Squad car hauled hubby off to jail but the wife had minor bruising and didn't want it to go any further. The best we could do was keep the hubby locked up for four hours and then recommend the wife go up to the hospital for a check over.

It's frustrating for me as a detective because domestic violence was one of those things, we were hot on but if the wife refused to press charges we were stymied.

We did note the callout in our incident report log so if the hubby did it again, we might be able to take our own action, but I knew this was not going anywhere. I had a couple more cases to deal with, so I went and interviewed the complainants - a burglary that was done by an amateur or a gang of kids. I said I'd sent the fingerprint boys around and went to the next case. Another burglary and I handled it in the same way as I had done the previous case. It's a fallacy that we have a team of experts on hand ready to jump in at the drop of a hat. For the most part we will send the fingerprint lads around and put the prints on file. If a felon has gotten away with a crime, they will likely try another one, or something more serious. Usually, when we catch a felon, we will look at our fingerprint files and we can often get them for more than one crime.

I had a late lunch with the Sarge and then I walked round to the top of Pukaki Street to see Jacko.

The walk round gave me a little time to think about how to handle Jacko. Do I go hardball or do I treat it as a genuine enquiry and give Jacko the chance to deny all knowledge of the drug dealing.

I decided to go to hardball. That way I could use the Boss's more aggressive interview tactics.

When we were sitting down in Jacko's office, I laid out the charges against his 'security men'. Jacko denied everything at first. When I told Jacko that I didn't come down with the last shower, he slightly changed his tune. Now it was more of a 'What can you do' scenario where it was so hard to get good security blokes that could deal with some of the homeless. If they had a little sideline going in drug dealing then what could he, as the Boss, do?

I used a trick that I had learned from the Boss. I didn't speak. The next one who speaks loses!

After a second or two of my silence, Jacko started again.

"Yeah, like I was saying. It's hard to get security men nowadays."

I replied, "So you get them from the Black Power mob. How do you get these guys through the security screening and such?" I then shut up.

Jacko knew he was in a very dangerous area for him. "Some of them start before the security screening, cause it's a national crisis, this homeless problem and stuff."

Again, I was careful with my words, "So you let them start with their drug dealing before you even start their security clearance." I was silent again.

To be honest I was more surprised that this type of questioning was working so well.

Jacko was in a mess of his own making. "Look, this homeless thing is a big issue for the people of Rotorua. We're doing the best that we can!"

I had to put in my piece. "So tell me, Jacko, do these guys just sell drugs to the homeless or do they have a larger clientele?"

At that Jacko was admitting defeat, "I'm not happy with your questions, Detective Sergeant, I should have a lawyer speaking for me."

"That is always an option for you, Jacko. Perhaps next time we'll have this interview at the station and then you can bring your lawyer with you."

With that I arose, and Jacko showed me out of his office. Very politely, I might add, but I'm sure he was pleased to see the back of me. For me, I was very pleased this new line of questioning was working out.

When I returned to our office, the Boss had just got back from Hamilton and the Sarge, and I and the Boss sat down for a brew.

I relayed what had happened with Jacko. I was quite pleased I had been able to get him on the back foot. The Boss was pleased but also a little frustrated. "I like what you did, initiative and stuff. But the CP and I are conducting our own look at Jacko's team of security blokes. That's one of the reasons why I asked the two DCs and the Squaddies to go for the front men only. Don't worry. You've done no damage and it won't hurt to for him to know we also have an eye on him, as well."

Feeling just a little deflated I asked the Boss how he had got on in Hamilton.

He was also pleased to change the subject, "They have got three Crown Prosecutors over there and they are all as good as the guy we have here. I watched this guy rip apart testimony from the gang of ram raiders like it was yesterday's newspaper. The only thing he had no control over was this stupid tart from the Youth Justice Department. Once she started on about poor backgrounds and stuff even the judge let her ramble on. Evidently, we have to let people like this ramble on or we end up with a retrial because they didn't get a chance to have someone speak on their behalf."

The Sarge interrupted, "So let's get this right. They managed to nick a couple of motors, pick out a target for a ram raid and set up a system for flogging all these fags, and they still get a retrial if they don't have some do gooders to speak on their behalf?"

The Boss replied," And don't forget, this do gooder is paid for with our tax dollars. Makes you wonder where we are going, doesn't it?"

Then the Boss turned his attention to matters at Rotorua.

"Right I had a phone call from the CP on my way back. I spoke to him about Carl Jeffries last week. He may have a cancelled trial date set in about three weeks. One day only, on Friday, if we can get all our paperwork over to him today, he'll pick and choose what he wants and send it back to us for us to tidy up. After that we have a few days, maybe a week for him to sort out his paperwork and then Carl Jeffries trial can go ahead. It's a straight plea deal so we can put in victim impact reports if we want. I'm going to suggest that we don't bother with the sexual assault, and we don't worry too much about the assault or GBH charges. If we're really picky we can go with victim impact report on the two murders he's charged with here in town. I'll let the lads in Auckland know about their murders and see if they want to do something, but it's a straight plea deal as far as we are concerned. Any questions? Right, let me have a first look at what we have for Carl Jeffries and then I'll let the DS have a once over. Right, let's get to it."

With that, the Boss went into his office with a mountain of paperwork on the Carl Jeffries trial and closed his door.

I spoke to the two DCs about my session with Jacko. They seemed pleased but deferred to the Boss and the CP having a go at Jacko through his lack of attention to the paperwork regarding his security men.

Just then I got a call from Otonga School. They asked me to go round and meet the grounds man on the soccer pitch at Springfield road. When I got there the grounds man and the headmaster were there. It seemed someone had sprayed weed killer in the goal mouth area at the far end. The grounds man was furious. Someone, over the weekend, had gone up to the soccer pitch and sprayed what looked like some type of weed killer on the penalty area. Most of the penalty area was starting to turn a bit brown. I immediately told the grounds man to section the pitch off. For the most part I had no clue about what had been sprayed on the area and I wanted to make sure it was nothing toxic to the kids that played there. The grounds man went off to get his rope and things for holding the rope up while I chatted to the headmaster. He reckoned there had been a game played on the pitch on Saturday morning so it had to have happened after Saturday lunch. I was not quite so certain. It may have been sprayed on the Friday night and there may well have been a game played on the pitch. I told the headmaster he would need to advise anyone who played on the pitch on the Saturday to go and get tested for any toxic chemicals. I got on the phone to the forensic lads and asked them to come round and take an analysis of the chemical used. The only way they could do that was to dig out a square foot of the turf in two or three places and then go back to the lab for their analysis. Okay, I get it's important for safety's sake, but the forensic lads turned up in their bio- hazard gear. As soon as the grounds man saw the forensic lads, he also wanted bio-hazard gear. He had to stop halfway through putting out the ropes and stays to put on his bio-hazard gear before completing his job. Then the forensic lads decided it would pay to be extra cautious so they and the grounds man completely fenced off the whole pitch. To be fair, the forensic lads were quite excited to have something different to work on and they agreed to work into the night to get us a result as soon as they could.

We didn't get the result until around 9.00 that night. It was a commercial type of spray used, readily available in any retail shop such as Bunnings or Miter 10. That didn't give me too much to work on but I thanked the lads in forensics for staying on at work.

I rang the headmaster and the grounds man and told them what we were up against. That reminded the headmaster there was another kids game due to be played on the ground the following day. He scurried off the phone and set about ringing whoever he could ring to cancel the game and reschedule it.

I rang the grounds man and told him what we knew. He immediately got snarky and said the entire penalty area would have to be re-laid. I immediately tried to get jokey with him and told him about the overtime he would make. He reckoned the school couldn't afford overtime and could barely pay his wages anyway. Oh, well, at least I tried!

Around 5pm I went home and had a quiet night. I watched a great documentary on Carlo Escobar, the drug king from Colombia. Part of me wanted to be among all these drug seizures on the Florida Coast and to be excited. And a bigger part of me was happy that I was a DS in sleepy little Rotorua. I always knew what I wanted in life, and I reckoned I had it pretty good here. I did get energized when the forensic lads rung me and I could tell what we were up against but I was left hanging on a limb once I had rung the headmaster and the grounds man. I was all annoyed and had nothing to vent my anger on. Who would do such a bloody stupid thing to a kids soccer pitch?

<u>Tuesday</u>

In the morning the Boss had me get on the phone to the maraes again. He wanted to get it done with and reckoned we should be talking to two marae per day. Although he did not yet have the paperwork back to me for the Carl Jeffries trial, he was the Boss, so I complied and rang the maraes up. As luck would have it, we were able to fit two maraes in for that day. The first one was in the morning and the second one was for the afternoon. I loved the casualness of the marae when they said they would be there all day so come when you are ready.

The first one of the day that we went to, the Boss made his apology, but the elder was not really concerned either way.. He had heard about what went down with the Council of but he seldom attended elder meetings. He accepted the Boss's apology and we talked for half an hour, but there was no information to be gleaned from this visit. In the afternoon we met one of the Elders who had been at the meeting. The atmosphere was a little cool but by the time we had sat and had another cup of tea we were fine.

Going back to the station, or our version of the station, the conversation was a little quiet. I figured that the Boss had something on his mind, so I was also happy to not speak. When we got back the Sarge told us he had heard that Jeff Whitely was negotiating to sell his business with the Insurance Agencies for over a half million dollars. According to the Sarge, negotiations were well advanced. The Boss asked him if he had heard anything from the other two Rotary members who had confessed to their involvement but as far as the Sarge knew the architect, Craig Mansell, was still trying to get a buyer and the lad from the garage on View Road was still hoping to get away with pleading to the court that his business was the sole income earner for his family and for the two guys that worked for him. He rather hoped that this approach may get him just parole for the assault rather than the murder which eventually happened. To be honest, I didn't hold out too much hope for him.

When we got back, the Boss had me on the phone to maraes again. I had little problem booking the next two and we finished the day discussing how we could improve our chances of getting more information out of the Elders.

Wednesday

The local paper's lead article was on the damage to the soccer pitch at Otonga School. Yes, they pondered the same question as I had, who would have done this to a kids' soccer pitch but the local rag took it to the next level Not only did they have a pic showing the damage but they also managed to get one of the school kids crying and by an amazing coincidence this kid, at just ten years old, had been a follower of the Wellington Phoenix for a few years and had long held the desire to be a professional soccer player when he grew up. Now the pitch was ruined he didn't know what to do to prolong his dreams anymore. I might be a bit blasé about the local papers actually finding out about a kid who had always been a follower of the Phoenix and who had always wanted to be a pro soccer player and was crying on demand. Maybe I am being just a teeny bit sarcastic about how they make up these stories.

The Sarge knew the Boss and I were busy visiting the maraes, so he took it on himself to hand out anything that he got from the Squaddies the previous night. With the Boss and I set for our first visit we did well, well sort of! This Elder had been at the ill-fated meeting with the Boss and had noticed me 'not giving his words my fullest attention.' We were subjected to how important lineage and whakapapa were, and then he proceeded to give me his full lineage back to when the canoes landed at Tauranga. At least that's what I think he recited. As his speech was predominantly using Māori words, I didn't really understand what he was talking about, so I nodded my head at what seemed appropriate moments. The Boss sat on my side of the table and made sure I didn't go to the land of nod by occasionally giving me a kick in the shins. It was probably only for about ten minutes and then it was the Boss's turn to give his apology. With honors done on both sides we then sat down and had a cup of tea. I'll give full credit to the Boss for how he casually introduces the topic of the marae lads being given a stern talking to or even worse. It was very skillfully done. As we listened to this guy speak, we discovered that in Māori legends it says that a person who is born at the time of Matariki is acknowledged to have a special talent or skills. Although he did not know of such a person it was a part of Māori folklore.

We thanked him for his kindness and hospitality, and we left. I think we may have mended a few fences with our visit, so we felt happy that we had achieved something.

Thursday

The next morning I was in at my usual time of around 7.30 and of course the Sarge was already in. Also tucked away in his office was the Boss. When I queried this with the Sarge, he said the Boss was already in when he got in at 7.15.

While I was over getting the coffees, the Boss walked out with his pile of paperwork and dropped it on the Sarge's desk. "Here you go, Sarge. Give that a look before we give it back to the DS. Then we can give it all over to the Crown Prosecutor so he can do his filing with the Courts."

It was at this point I walked back in with the coffees, so we all sat down, including the two DCs, and had our coffee while we went over our day. The two DCs had nothing new to add to their paperwork so were ready to give it to the CP. The Boss and I were heading out to the maraes again and I had made two appointments the previous day. When it was the Sarge's turn, he merely looked at the pile of paperwork the Boss had dumped on his desk and said, "Well, I'll think of something that will keep me busy for the rest of the day!"

With that we set about our day. I thought it was a little bit of a bore going out to see these decent blokes who may or may not have been a part of our investigations, but the Boss was quite chirpy as he felt that at the least it would keep the ACI happy that we were going out and meeting these guys on the marae. I reckon the Boss was going on about the mana that it must give to himself and me, but I felt it might be more about this being a huge benefit for the big Boss.

When we arrived at the next marae we were formally greeted and welcomed on to the marae. Once we sat down and the Boss's formal apology was made, then we were offered a brew. So far so good.

Obviously, I let the Boss do the talking and he eventually brought up the subject of getting the youngsters on the marae to follow the traditions of the marae.

This time the guy was a little more animated. We spoke about 'kids of today' and all they want to do is 'play on their games' etc. This guy went on about how these kids needed a bit more respect in their lives. Before we knew it, we were talking about giving the kids some discipline. Sometimes a stern word was needed. At other times they needed a hiding which was probably the first hiding they had ever got in their lives.

As for me, I was content to let the Boss lead the conversation while I tried to take mental notes.

The Boss left this Elder to carry on while he spoke about the kids on the marae who needed a lesson in the old ways of doing things and respect for the Elders etc. Okay, the Boss occasionally prodded the guy to go a certain way or to follow a certain line that the Boss thought he wanted covered.

This guy told us pretty much most of what we wanted to know. Yes, there was a guy who arranged for the youth of today to get a talking to. Yes, the same guy also stepped in if the kids needed a good hiding. He had no idea of how this was sorted out, or how money was paid to get the kids back into line. But he did think it was a good idea and this mystery guy sorted it all out for them.

We agreed it was hard to deal with the kids of today and when we felt he had vented enough we thanked him for his troubles and for meeting with us.

All in all, I'd say we had a very fruitful morning session, and the Boss was quite chirpy when we drove back to town.

When we had lunch with the Sarge in town we relayed as much of what the guy had to say as we could, and the Sarge agreed that it confirmed what we had discussed with the Elders Committee. Debate took place about who or how we could track this mystery man down. Nothing came from this discussion beyond hoping we might get lucky with the next marae, or the one after that or, etc. I also got a call from the grounds man at the Otonga School. He asked me how long he had to wait before he re-laid the turf on the soccer pitch. I suggested he ring the forensic lads to get a better answer.

Within a few minutes he was back on the phone to me saying the forensic lads had told him at least a fortnight. I said that sounded about right. I think he wanted me to countermand the forensics lads' say so. He was quite disappointed when I reckoned the forensics lads were about right.

In the afternoon we had a session with another marae. I don't quite know what it is but once you get on a roll, the ball keeps on rolling. Again the Boss made a formal apology and we sat down for a cup of tea. The Boss did his thing and steered the chat the way he wanted it to go. This guy was just like the one earlier in the day. He had a thing about the kids on the marae not respecting the Elders in a proper manner. With the Boss's prodding he mentioned the Matariki man. Only this time he was saying that this guy is a real guy. I didn't quite know whether to believe him as maybe he also thinks Santa Claus is real, but I continued to be the quiet observer.

The Boss took a more proactive approach. He asked how this guy contacted him. The Elder carried on by saying that when it is agreed that a kid needs a talking to or a good hiding it is agreed by the Elders, and it just happens. Naturally the Boss probed a little further by asking does this Matariki man get paid and the guy sort of clammed up. Maybe he thought he had said too much? With us not getting anything further from this Elder we thanked him for his hospitality and welcome and then we left.

On the way home, the Boss was musing aloud, and I was keeping up my end of the chat. He reckoned that this Matariki guy was actually a real guy within the marae circle, and he organised for the assaults and the good bollocking (The Boss's words, not mine). How do we find out who this bloke is, and how does he get paid etc. By the time we got back to our office we had decided that we could only hope we got lucky with the other marae Elders. We told the Sarge of our progress so far and then the Boss left me to tee up our appointments for the next day.

Friday

The Sarge was still doing his thing with the calls from over the road so anything that wanted CIB input was given to the two DCs and the Boss and I were left alone to visit the maraes.

Well Friday was a bust. We got nothing out of no-one. Whether it was just bad luck or whatever, no one was admitting knowing about this Matariki man. On the way back the Boss asked me if I minded working a Saturday. Perhaps we could do a couple more maraes. It was a while since I had seen the Boss keen to go out on a Saturday and with him being the Boss, of course I caved in and agreed to it.

Once back at the Nick I set out to tee up our meetings for the Saturday. Fortunately I was able to get one booked for 10 am and one booked for 'around midday'. I quite like the Māori attitude to time. It's a very flexible thing with them.

The Sarge was surprised that we were coming in on a Saturday while he was at home having a lie-in but that was what you did when you had a Boss like mine. Also, I knew that the Boss would give us a day off in lieu, sometime in the future, when he remembered.

Saturday

As the Boss got a better rate for using his vehicle we usually travelled out in his motor, and at least he picked me up from my place.

When we got to the next marae for our appointment, we were formally greeted by perhaps a dozen Elders or friends of the Elders. Straight away we knew we would not be having a cozy chat with perhaps just one person. These people were here to hear the Boss apologise. Initially, I thought the day would be a bust for our investigations, but it turned out better than expected. As well as the formal greeting we were also given food. If you've never had the opportunity to have a feed on a marae, you are missing something. Yes, the food may be fairly basic, but it is made with love and respect and you somehow get that in the taste buds. I can't describe it any other way, but it is a way of sharing your thoughts and feelings with the greater marae family. During the lunch, the Boss and I were separated, and we each had our own locals to talk with. The Boss was feeding his face well when I glanced over at him. Well it is a sign of disrespect to your host if you don't participate enthusiastically. I got down to talking with a group of Elders who I managed to steer around to the reason for our visit. I was spoken to by all of these people and I can't really remember who said what, but I did find out the following snippets when I asked about Matariki. Evidently the full name of Matariki is "Nga Mata o te Ariki Tawhiramatea". Translated that means 'The Eyes of the God Tawhiramatea.' In other countries we would call it the "Pleiades."

In Māori tradition it symbolizes that the God of wind, Tawhiramatea, was so angry when his siblings separated his parents (Ranginui, the sky father and Papatuanuku the earth mother) that he tore out his eyes and threw them into the heavens. Hence, the Pleiades. I heard somewhere that in some countries they are called the 'Seven Sisters', but I digress.

I found all of this fascinating and to have it all explained by my fellow hosts was quite an experience for me. I have to say that although we may scoff as superstition at this legend, we believe that Moses parted the Red Sea. I say no more on the matter.

We had to say farewell to this lovely bunch as we had to get to our next appointment. We did not arrive until nearly 1.30pm but nothing was actually said. We did explain that our previous hosts had made us so welcome that it would have been impolite to scurry off. With that being said, someone in the background gave the word that they should provide us with afternoon tea and so we had another feast of fresh baking to deal with. We were allowed to sit together at this Marae, and I listened as the Boss skillfully tried to turn the conversation around to what we were after - more info about this supposed 'Matariki man'. We didn't get that much out of our hosts, and I rather got the impression they were a subtribe of the main Hapu/Family group, by that I mean that they were not really kept in the loop, as it were.

All in all a brilliant day if not for the waistline, and in my mind, I remembered Sarge's words about the yearly physicals coming up soon. Oops!

The Boss dropped me off at home and said he'd see me bright and early on Monday morning. Obviously, that meant I would be in on Monday. I thought about ringing the Sarge to keep him updated but then thought better of it and left him alone. I settled into my weekend of relaxation and mentally went over what we had achieved this week. We had made some progress, but it was all of a somewhat abstract nature with nothing definite to get our hopes up. After that I forgot about work and spent a lazy weekend catching up with Sky Sport. Halfway through Saturday night I decided I should go for a jog in the morning. I also had the same thought on Sunday evening. Somehow, I didn't manage to jog. There's always next week.

Chapter 10

Monday

Monday morning. A beautiful day. I regretted that I had not managed a jogging session over the weekend. Got into work at my usual time. Sarge was already there. I didn't ask him if he went for a jog but if he asked me, I would be prepared to lie!

The Boss came in just after 8.00, by which time the two DCs were already in. While I waited for my coffee to be delivered, I realised that both DCs were still in the office and waiting for their coffees as well. The Sarge managed a few choice words and one of them scuttled off. It's always best not to keep the Sarge waiting for his coffee.

The Boss joined us as we sat round and planned our day. The Sarge only had a couple of items to pass on to the CIB and the Boss delegated them out to the two DCs.

The two DCs had another couple of suspects, arriving at a motel, picked up by the Squad cars. We had a burglary in Springfield reported and an assault case. As the Boss and I were still working our way through the list of outstanding maraes, the Boss sent Dave Powell to attend to the motel drug dealer and Tim Cross to handle the report of the break-in in Springfield. He set me to tee up a couple of appointments with maraes and then he disappeared into his office and spent the next half hour on the phone.

I also got a call from the grounds man at Otonga School. He asked me if I had any break throughs with the case. I had to tell him that no we hadn't but were following up some promising leads. He asked me what they were so I told him they had to remain confidential until they could be given to the papers. He would have preferred I'm sure than me saying I had been more preoccupied with the marae visits!

The Sarge was still going over the paperwork for the Carl Jeffries case when I mentioned that the papers were supposed to be with the CP by Friday. He grumbled something at me which I missed, as he closed his door and then I went to call my list.

We did well on Monday. Two more maraes down. Both of which were quite talkative, with our assistance and guidance. We definitely did get the impression that this Matariki guy was actually a real person. He could seemingly organise a hiding or a stern talking to when required. What we didn't quite get was a name we could follow up on. We also got the impression that the people we spoke to were active members of the Elders Committee.

Also, as an aside, I should mention that of all of the maraes we visited, four of them said that the Māori version of Te Tiriti was the only one to go with, three said the Pakeha version was the best one to go with, and five said that the Treaty was a poorly worded document and given today's more diverse population, was not a document that could be relied on one way or the other. I put that point in and then I will move on.

Driving back to the office, the Boss was in a good mood. We had seemingly established that this 'Matariki man' existed and was a real person. We hadn't got any further with the identity of this guy, but we would assume that the 'Matariki man' was of Māori descent, and we needed to get the marae visits tidied up so we could actually get on with other work. Our other work was mainly little bits and pieces and scut work, but it was still there in the background and would need to be acted on when we were finished with the visits. I also mentioned that the Sarge was still trying to sort his way through the Carl Jeffries case. The Boss was disappointed. Very disappointed! Evidently that paperwork should have been with the CP by today. He had marked a point or two that I could well work on and no doubt the Sarge would probably find a few things to advance the case. He decided that I should stay in the office on Tuesday and work on the Carl Jeffries case. At the very least I should get it to the Crown Prosecutor by the close of play on Tuesday.

When I queried that the ACI wanted me to go on the visits, the Boss simply said, 'What he doesn't find out about, won't kill him.' With that being said the Boss set up his own visits for the Tuesday and left me and the Sarge to work on the Jeffries case.

Tuesday

The Boss had set me a couple of points to rework on the Jeffries Case and the Sarge had found another three examples where I might have used different tenses or something. Between the Sarge and I we had it all sorted out by midafternoon on the Tuesday, and I walked the case file up to the CP's office on Arawa St.

The CP was quite a relaxed sort of guy when you saw him in his office, although he had a reputation for being fiery in the court if his opposition took him lightly. When I handed him the file he flicked through it and said thank you. I suppose we are all professionals in our own field. The Sarge and I had gone through the file with a fine toothcomb and the CP just said it looked fine. No doubt I would hear from him if there was anything he wanted to fine tune.

When I got back to the office, the Boss had already returned from his afternoon session on the marae, and he had some news. "This 'Matariki man' is a real person! He was born on the new year, the Māori new year, that is. The first thing the dad saw when he walked outside of the hospital was the Pleiades, you know, the stars of Matariki. and he took that as an omen. Named his kid after the whole Matariki thing. Okay, it might take a bit of digging but we have the lad!"

The Sarge was delighted and so was I! The Boss had got one of the Elders he had seen to really relax and the Boss had literally just sat back while the Elder had spoken about our 'Matariki man'. The Elder had said he had known this 'Matariki man' all of his life and had even taught him about things when he was a young boy. He even said that this youngster had needed stern talking to when he was young bloke, although he never needed a good beating. He had learned his lessons quite quickly. One thing this friendly Elder did not give us was the guy's name! When pressed for more the Elder said that this guy was doing a service and it would not be right to tell us anymore.

I couldn't quite see what the Boss was so joyous about. In Rotorua we had a population of Māori of around 30%. Doing my quick math's I reckoned we had a total population of perhaps 70,000 people. Given that, it would be a Māori population of around 25,000. Given that half would be female and half of them would need to be aged at least 25 or older, we were looking for a needle in around 4 or 5 thousand male Māori's!

The Sarge also pointed out the flaw in the Boss's thinking, "Boss, I reckon you're still looking for one person in about five thousand. What do you suggest we do? Check the records for anyone with a birthday between May and August that somehow has the name of Tawhiramatea? What if he is called 'the eyes of Tawhiramatea?' And is that enough to pull him in for questioning?"

When the Sarge was pulling something down, he really pulled it down! I was almost sorry to see the Boss looking so happy one minute and disappointed the next.

The Boss seemed a little short with the Sarge, "I never said it would be easy, did I?" before he walked into his office.

The Boss re-emerged from his office and told me to tee up our visits for the next day. I had hoped I would be let off the visits, but it seemed like I was back on them!

Wednesday

On Wednesday our first visit was out towards the airport, perhaps a 15-minute ride. We were greeted on to the marae by the guy who was waiting for us. Sometimes it's a formal welcome with chanting and singing (Waiata) and the hongi and sometimes it's a lot more casual.

The Boss had asked me to leave the speaking to him and I was more than pleased to oblige. Once the formalities of the apology were over, we all sat down for a cup of tea. That was when the Boss really excelled. He quickly brought up the subject of 'kids of today' having no respect for Elders and settled back to listening. This Elder was an old school Māori guy. A nice guy but open like a book. He knew we were there to find out more about this 'Matariki man' and he just about said 'ask me what you want to know.' What we learned from this guy was a whole heap of minor facts about our man of mystery.

Age: 'Only his contact on the marae Elders would know that'

He's a Māori Bloke: 'Obviously. A woman would not be trusted with such an important decision'.

Um, where does he work? "Again, only his contact would know that. The Elders will decide, as a group, if a person needs a talking to and then it happens. Someone on the committee makes a phone call and it will happen in the next day or so.'

Does it cost the Elders money for this guy to operate? 'Oh yes, but it's a Koha thing.'

And what does that cost, for the Koha: 'Koha is always a gift for a service. For a good talking to it might cost perhaps $500.'

And for a young lad that is misbehaving; 'Usually it would cost perhaps $1500. I understand the 'Matariki man' may use extra help for this. But I don't know any details that would be of help to you.'

The Elder said a few more things about our' Matariki man' but it was fairly general stuff.

As we drove back to the station the Boss was in a pensive but talk out loud kind of mood. He was asking for my opinion but also not asking. I think I answered what he wanted. By the time we got back to the office the Boss had decided to get the two DC's working on going through our 'Client base' to look for anyone with the name of Tawhiramatea or the eye of Tawhiramatea or anything that sounded like that or the Māori version of that. I helpfully suggested they use sort characteristics or search parameters. When they looked at me quizzically, I suggested they look it up and then they would learn about it.

I have to say that both the Boss and the Sarge looked at me as if I didn't really know what I was on about. But I bluffed my way through them all.

As we pulled into the carpark at the back of our office, the Boss noticed that most of the parking reserved for the Police had been taken. Knocking on the back door of the office the Boss was already working out what to say to the guys who were busy moving in as our new neighbours.

The Boss was already cutting through to the office next door when the Sarge asked him if he would like the Sarge to also join him. The Boss declined the Sarge's offer even as the Sarge said," It won't go well if you go in there like a bull at a gate."

As the Boss disappeared through our front door, the Sarge continued with his comment, "Because you're not the most tactful when you're in this mood and they are all lawyers."

It must have no more than five minutes later when the Boss reappeared muttering to himself.

The Sarge, because he was not officially under the Boss's guidance, asked politely, "So how did your explanation of the carparking go?"

The Boss disappeared into his office with the comment trailing behind him. Then he reappeared standing halfway out of his office. "Every damn sleazebag that couldn't make it into a decent law firm is parked right next door to us. And this Sheila who is only a law executive asked me to wait while she got a lawyer out to explain the new parking arrangements. Next thing I'm fronted by Craig Mills and Terry Hohepa who have come out to meet the new neighbours."

The Sarge pointed to an envelope on his desk. "Do you think now is a good time to take this in?"

When I enquired what 'this is', the Sarge replied, "They're having a drinkies do to open the new office on Friday night. We're all invited, as is the ACI. When I rang the ACI this morning, he indicated it was compulsory for us all to attend. He will also be there, but I have been excused the need to wear my uniform, unless I particularly want to."

My reply was that I might leave it for an hour before I mentioned it to the Boss. When he was in this kind of mood he was better left alone.

The Boss emerged from his office at around 1.30. We were supposed to meet our next marae Elder at 2.00. The Boss had gotten over his bad mood so when the Sarge offered to give him the Invite to next door's drinks, I shook my head. It's always best not have the Boss in another iffy mood when he is going to visit a marae.

Well, the next visit went well. At least it confirmed most of what was said by the guy from that morning. He also added a few more snippets of info but nothing that would clearly identify our mystery 'Matariki man'.

We left and returned to the office which is when the Sarge handed over the Invite along with the comment that the ACI had made it compulsory. The Boss was not well pleased, but he gave it back to the Sarge. The Boss asked if the Sarge was going. When the Sarge replied that he was included in the invite, but the ACI had indicated he would prefer the Sarge to be in civvies, the Boss merely replied that the Sarge should go in uniform. That it might make half of the people in the room decide on an early night.

I arranged for the last few marae visits to take place. We would be all over and done with the visits by Friday with a little luck.

The two DCs were busy working their way through our 'client base' but as yet had come up with nothing that showed of any interest.

Nothing really happened on the remaining marae visits. Some points on the identity of the 'Matariki man' were confirmed but we still had nothing we could work with.

As far as I was concerned, we were at least done with the visits. It had taken the best part of a fortnight to get it done and we were only a little bit ahead of where we were before we started. We knew the guy existed. We believed he was born under the Matariki skies. He organised for the miscreants on various maraes to be brought back into line. He was paid for doing his dirty work by the Elders of the committee of Elders. That was about all that we knew.

The Boss called in the two DCs who were still working on the 'client base'. They had nothing to report. Any person they could have nominated had an alibi for a part of the time. If you read that as 'locked up' it should be a little clearer. They were probably 80% of the way through the 'client base' so he left them to continue.

On the Friday morning we were sat with our coffee. The Boss and I still had one more visit to tidy up and we were done. The two DCs had finished on the 'client base' with no success and the Sarge reminded us we had the visit to our new neighbours to go through on the Friday evening. I'm sure there were other bits and pieces of petty crimes that we had to work with, but we weren't exactly feeling flushed with success.

The Boss remembered he had his weekly meeting with the ACI set for that morning, so he rang and deferred it until the afternoon. The big Boss wasn't thrilled until the Boss told him it was all due to the last visit to the marae Elders and then he was a little mollified.

I asked the Boss if he was going to mention this 'Matariki man' to the Boss and he said he wasn't going to mention it until they were a bit closer to the identity. I also reckoned he wasn't going to mention anything about the Boss having a slightly ulterior motive for being so keen to visit the marae Elder Committee. The Big Boss was getting very positive feedback from our visits to the maraes around town and thought it showed the Force in a positive light. It also might have shown the big Boss in a more positive light as well, but we don't mention that aspect.

The Boss and I went on our last visit to the marae which was the Marae at Ohinemutu. That might have been another reason to not mention it to the Boss. He probably would have wanted to come with us, being a local boy made good etc.

We met with Mason at the marae. I liked Mason, he was a no-nonsense kind of guy who you could talk to without inadvertently giving an offense to. He accepted the Boss's apology and then we sat and talked for a while. Nothing came out about our 'Matariki man', which I did not expect to happen in any case. However, fences had been mended and we were all pleasant to each other.

We returned to the office and had a late lunch and then the Boss went over to see the big Boss for their weekly meeting. I sat with the Sarge and talked about his plans for getting his boat and where he could keep it at this place in Huia St until I got a call from the CP's office asking me to call over for a meeting.

With nothing planned I said I'd come right over and have a session with the CP.

I was probably there for the best part of an hour and the CP really just wanted to go over the minutiae of the case. He reckoned that Carl had got off lightly with 15 years now that he had all of the details of the case. For me, I was happy to have a case where we had discovered the murderer and his three associates. Or three of his possibly ten associates is probably a better way of putting it.

With that I wandered back to the office. The Boss was back also by now. He reckoned I should leave and get ready for the festivities for the evening. He had some paperwork to tidy up, but he would also go off early if he got the chance. The Sarge was the only one who really had to stay until the office closed at five. Then he would shoot home and get changed. Despite the Boss's recommendation he was going to go home and change. We all agreed to meet back at the rear of our office at 6.15 and go into the new neighbours as a group. I think the invitation had said 6.00 but none of us wanted to appear too keen.

I wandered off home and had a leisurely shower, sat around and then got changed into my 'non office 'wear. By 6.00 I was on the road and ready.

By 6.15 only the Sarge was running a little late which was unusual for him. He arrived and we walked around the front of Fenton St and entered the new offices as a group.

I have to say I was surprised at how well the place had been done up. It was a biggish sized office, but it had a reception area, four conference rooms complete with the law books you always see in Law Offices and then it had smaller almost cubicle sized areas out the back for the various solicitors or barristers to have their own individual desk. Everything you needed to look like you were a big firm but in reality, it was just a group of ten or a dozen legal eagles trying to look a little posher than they were. And, of course, being right across the road from the bright and shiny new Cop shop they were in a prime place to pick up new business.

The big Boss was there in civvies. I don't think I'd ever seen him out of uniform, but there he was. He did moan to the Boss about everybody in our group being late. I believe the Boss might have mentioned we were all working on a big case and that it was unavoidable. I knew most of the people at the drinkies do and I managed to mingle nicely, along with the Sarge. The two principles of the new office came over and spoke to me and the Sarge for the allotted three minutes and then we were moved on to lesser lights in the new enterprise.

At one point, the Sarge whispered urgently 'Hohepa and Mills. Your six o'clock'.

Because they were coming from behind me, I didn't realise it until Terry Hohepa and his mate, something or other Mills were standing in front of me. Naturally I shook their hands and congratulated them on their new office structure. I might have added that it was very impressive, which it was, if you hadn't seen the room out the back with all of the Cubicles.

"A new Era," said Hohepa. Then he added, "And so good to see you Sergeants out for the evening. Thank you for coming."

The Sarge was very quick to correct our learned friend. "It's actually Detective Sergeant and Senior Sergeant" then after the briefest pause he added "Terry".

There was a momentary pause before Terry Hohepa replied, "Yes, it's so good to see you both Detective Sergeant and Senior Sergeant. If you will excuse us, we are told we must circulate and there is the Mayor. Hello there," he said out loud as he looked for further notables to make sure he was noticed.

With that we were effectively dismissed. The Sarge said," I don't why it is, but that sod always gets me riled."

I replied that I thought the Sarge was ahead on points and when did he get Senior Sergeant.

"Oh, that it came through a few weeks ago but they give it out with a box of cornflakes nowadays."

I knew full well that it wasn't given out with a box of cornflakes. First you had to pass a theory exam and then go through a fairly rigorous verbal barrage where they tried to trip you up. If the Sarge was now a Senior Sergeant, he would have had to work for it. "Well, congratulations anyway. It's no more than you deserve having to put up with the rubbish I keep coming up with." I was genuinely thrilled that he had made it. Then that got me thinking it was probably something I should be going for. Maybe after the yearly physicals?

I sidled over to the Boss with the inevitable question, "How long do we have to stay before we can head off?"

The Boss replied, with a nod to someone in the distance, "At least another half hour and then it will be OK. Fancy a drink at the Caravel afterwards. You and the Sarge? Maybe the DCs."

"Done!"

"Have you spoken to Terry yet."

"No, Make that yes. He insulted the Sarge and me and then buggered off. Oh, did you hear the Sarge made it to Senior Sarge?"

"Sod it, that's a good enough reason for me. Round up the Sarge and we'll ease on out of here."

With that, we headed off down to the Caravel and got just a little tiddly. The main reason was that Sarge had made it to the next rank. Other than that, the Boss had decided we had put in some good work recently and it was time the boys went for a blowout. To be fair, we may have all got more than just a little bit tiddly! At some point in the evening the Boss made a phone call. When the Squad car arrived at the Caravel, the Boss asked the Squaddie to breathalyse him. Obviously, the Boss was over the limit, so the Boss organised for the Squaddie to give us all a lift home. Maybe it was an abuse of power or maybe it was a really good way to keep a few drunks off the road.

I had the whole weekend to recover from my excesses. On Sunday I mowed my lawn which inflicted a little more damage on me than it should have done, but by Monday I was still in bright and early.

<u>Monday</u>

The Boss was also in bright and early and headed off to Hamilton. I was surprised as he had not said he would be heading back there soon. Come to think of it, we didn't see much of the Boss for the next three days.

The Sarge came in on the Monday, all bright eyed and bushy tailed. He'd enjoyed the Friday night session with the five of us. He made a mention that we should think about doing it more often. That's when the Boss said he was headed up to Hamilton and got in his car.

None of us had known about the Hamilton trip so it was down to me to allocate the duties for the two DCs and myself.

One drug supplier in for the weekend, a domestic assault, two burglaries and a ram raid on a dairy in the Ford Block.

I took the domestic assault and one of the burglaries, and handed off the other jobs.

My domestic assault was always going to be an issue of getting the wife to press charges, which she wouldn't. I convinced her to get up to the hospital for a check over. I had to assure her that hospital had seen it all before and she wouldn't be forced into pressing charges.

The burglary looked a little iffy. Someone had too much knowledge of the occupants' habits. Either it was an inside job, or it was one of the neighbours. I knocked on a few doors around the vicinity and came up with a likely candidate. There was nothing I could do as there were no prints or anything to work with. I told the likely offender that I would be putting extra patrols in the area and after that there was not a lot I could do.

I gave DC Cross a call. He was working on the ram raid at the dairy on Ford Road. I called round to back him up, but it was very similar to the raids in Hamilton. I rather hoped they would not be moving to Rotorua from Hamilton. Given that DC Cross was probably more experienced at ram raids I left him to it and went back to the office. On my way back my phone rang, and it was a case from the Squaddies. It seems I have to go to John Paul School and see the headmaster. I drove up to John Paul School and I was glad I didn't have to worry about seeing the head master any more. There may have been a couple of times in my past where a visit to the headmaster's office might have involved me getting six of the best.

The headmaster met me in the carpark and took me out to see the groundman, Peter. They had received a late-night visitor who had done to the Cricket wicket what someone had done to the Otonga School a week or so before.

Obviously, it was a smaller area, but it would appear they had used the same amount of weed killer and done more damage. I told the groundsman to do the same as I told the Otonga School guy and fence it all off. I had the forensics lads come round with all of their bio-hazard gear and take away samples. Annoyingly I thought this may be the start of a new trend. The groundsman went away and returned with his ropes and stays. The forensics lads said they wanted a wider perimeter. I left them arguing and told the headmaster I would be in contact once I had a report from the forensics lads.

If it was a new trend, I was worried. Anyone spraying random chemicals on to a kids play area has to be a concern. I left it until I heard from the forensics lads.

Fortunately, the lads did not work into the night and it was the next morning before I got their report.

Nothing really happened for the next couple of days. The only bit of excitement I received was a call from the Boss on Wednesday asking me to leave the Thursday afternoon free. No explanation but I confirmed I was available and went back to solving, or working on, the petty crime that goes on in a city like Rotorua. Believe me the crims had been polite in leaving the days I had been visiting the maraes fairly crime free. Now they were back to their usual tricks.

<u>Thursday</u>

On Thursday morning the Boss was back in the office and I tried to get him to reveal what he wanted me for that afternoon. He was a little secretive and just asked me to wait.

At around two o'clock he got me up from my desk and told me to go on through to the interview room. When I got into the Interview room, I was alone for a few moments. I was almost wondering what the hell I had done and why was I being interviewed. After a moment or two the Boss walked in with Terry Hohepa, the lawyer from our next-door neighbours. I fully expected Terry Hohepa to walk in with a client he was representing but it didn't happen.

Another unusual thing. Under normal circumstances the Boss and I would sit on one side of the table while the client and his brief would sit on the other side. Not this time! The Boss pulled his chair around to the end of the table and sat down. If the Boss was playing his mind games with Terry, he had not mentioned it to me.

We all sat down and waited for the Boss to speak. The Boss started with. "That was a nice evening, last Friday night. You have got some flash offices in your new place, Terry."

Terry replied, "Is that what we are here for. To talk about our new décor? Perhaps you can borrow our architect and spruce up your own office, Detective."

The Boss was particularly unfazed by what I thought was a snarky reply by Terry.

"Now, Terry, you do know it's Detective Inspector Woods. Let's keep it formal."

Terry sat back. He folded his arms and waited. I won't say he was surly. It was more like he was just a little bit arrogant.

The Boss continued. He turned to me and spoke, "While you were annoying the good people of this city on Friday night, Detective Sergeant, I happened to have the chance to speak to Mr Hohepa's father." He turned to Terry and said, "He's a nice bloke. Very chatty. He was quite proud of what you had achieved in our town."

Terry looked just a little confused. He couldn't quite work out where the DI was going with this.

Turning back to me, the Boss continued, "I was looking at Terry's Law certificate hanging in the office at the front. I did notice that Terry's middle name was Pleiades and I thought to myself, that is an unusual name. So, I had a chat with Terry's Dad. It turns out that Terry was born under the New Year's Star cluster. Sorry, I should say the Māori new year. When Terry was born his dad went outside and the first thing, he saw was the Matariki Stars all shining away. He wanted to call his newborn son something to do with the Māori new year. Evidently the Elders of his Marae put the kybosh on that. It was something to do with not calling his son anything like the Gods or something like that. He settled on Pleiades because that was more of a Pakeha word and the Elders were happy enough with that. Have I got that right, Terry?"

Terry was just a little uncomfortable with this way of talking at an interview. He was more used to him being the brief and telling his client he should not answer that question etc. Terry replied, "Yes, I suppose so but what on earth does this have to do with me? Surely, I am not on trial for having a pakeha name. What about Terence?"

The Boss smiled, 'Okay Terry, I'll get round to it in a moment."

Turning back to me, he continued, "You remember how we've been searching for this 'Matariki man' for a few weeks?"

I assumed the Boss did not wish to be interrupted so I just nodded at his query.

"Well, I got to do some thinking over the weekend, and I had a hunch, very useful things, hunches. It got me to thinking I should go over to Hamilton and see our mate in Waikeria. Turns out he got an infection in his stab wound so he was still in Waikato Hospital. He's not complaining, because he still gets the Sky TV in Hamilton Hospital. Where was I? Oh Yes. At Waikato I wanted to ask our friend Carl Jeffries if he had anything to do with beating up the lads on the maraes. Turns out he did have a hand in most of them and reckoned he had been involved with at least five of them."

Turning to Terry Hohepa he said, "He reckons you were good for business, Terry. He also said he still got a grand for a good hiding when he had to come down here. That's another mystery. The Elders reckoned they gave you $1,500 but I'll get back to that."

Turning back to me he continued. I could see that Terry Hohepa was not thrilled with the way this was going but I was still trying to get my head round what the Boss was saying. I Had a good idea that we were about to get Terry Hohepa for something, but what it was I didn't know.

"Yeah, anyway this gave me a bit of a problem. Carl Jeffries reckoned he already had a deal with our Crown Prosecutor. When I tried to explain to him that was only for what we already knew, He said he would deny everything if it wasn't included in the 15-year maximum term he had already agreed to."

I could see Terry Hohepa out of the corner of my eye, and he seemed to perk up a little with this news.

The Boss continued, "Like I said, I now had a problem. I had to come all the way back to town to see the CP and see if we could include Carl's latest visits to our fair city on the existing agreement. The CP was adamant he would want another year at least, if not two years. He mentioned something about under privileged youth and all that stuff. I went home to do a bit of thinking and I was in before the Crown Prosecutor got into his office on the Tuesday. Fortunately, I have a great relationship with his PA. She's also called Jane, the same as the Boss's PA. Small world, isn't it. So, she told me that the CP would be in before 8.30 because he had a case that morning in the High court."

I could see that the Boss was trying to rile Terry Hohepa with his line of talking rather than asking questions, and it certainly seemed to be working.

Terry Hohepa had been silent up to this point as the Boss relayed the news to me. Now he spoke up. "Is there any real need for me to here for this charade, Detective Inspector?"

The Boss turned to Terry and said, "Me and the Detective Sergeant have spent the last two or three weeks finding out about this mysterious 'Matariki man'. So, yes, Terry, there is a need for you to be here. Besides, I look good in all this, so it's like a learning curve for the DS."

Turning back to me, the Boss continued, "I thought I'd try anything I could on the CP to see if I could change his mind. We needed Carl Jeffries to be a witness for our case against Terry, here. In the end I negotiated something of a deal with him. If I could get Carl Jeffries to agree to one extra year would the CP agree to allow parole after twelve years. We settled on parole after fourteen years and that got me back in my motor and heading up to Waikato Hospital, again.

Carl had not considered he might be eligible for parole, so he was fairly happy to accept that deal."

Terry Hohepa had had enough, "Detective Inspector, either charge me or am I free to go?"

The Boss was quite matter of fact when he responded to Terry's ultimatum. Reaching into his jacket pocket he pulled out a charge sheet which had been prepared by the Crown Prosecutor. "Okay, If you insist. Terrence Pleiades Hohepa, you are hereby charged with the following offences under the Crimes act..." The Boss formally charged him with being an accessory to assault and also for profiting from the assault by keeping a part of the proceeds of what he had been paid by the Elders. Then he gave him the standard warning that anything he may say could be taken down and used as evidence, etc. He was being very careful to do everything by the book. After all, this was a smart lawyer we were setting ourselves up against.

I don't think Terry was quite prepared for the Boss actually charging him. Perhaps he expected a few days grace to prepare his answers etc, but it was out there. He had now been formally charged. The Boss continued, "As of this moment you are formally charged and will be held in the cells over the road, until you are able to attend a hearing for a possible bail plea in the morning." Terry's face was a picture. It managed a look of shock along with a look of disbelief. Disbelief perhaps that he had been caught, I don't know, but the Boss waited for Terry to respond. After a few seconds the Boss added "Terrence Pleiades Hohepa. Do you understand these charges as I have read them, and do you have anything you would want to say."

Terry merely nodded uncertainly which the Boss made a note of and then, turning to me, he continued," So I hit Carl Jeffries up for the new deal and he was a starter for that. Oh, and you know how I don't get the Rotorua Review until usually on the Monday with me living out on Dansey Road, I had the brainwave of taking the Review with me for Carl on the Tuesday. There was a whole write up on the new neighbours with all of their mug shots on it. Everyone was included, even the receptionist was there. I thought I'd show it to Carl on my visit on the Tuesday. Straight away he picked our accused out of a line-up of maybe a dozen or more photos in the write up. It seems that he and Terry had met on two occasions. No, It was three occasions, wasn't it, Terry. You met once when you fingered a mark for him. For the Panel? Seems you called yourself the' Matariki man' that time, as well."

Now the Boss was intimating that Terry may have been involved with the 'Panel's' work as well.

Terry was quick with his reply," You've already questioned me about this 'Panel's 'work. It didn't go that well, as I recall."

The Boss was looking at Terry when he spoke, "Don't worry, Terrence. If I thought I could get you for that, I would have charged you with that as well. But you did call yourself the 'Matariki man' when you met Carl. I don't know if the name will work in your favour or not. Maybe it will give you a name when you're doing time. Whatever."

Turning back to me he continued, "Where was I? Oh Yes. I met with the Crown Prosecutor on the Tuesday afternoon, but it was quite late. We got the new plea deal typed up because Carl always wants things to be tidy before he will own up to anything. On the Wednesday I was back up to see Carl. Did I tell you he is back in Waikeria, now? Anyway, his infection is ok to be dealt with by antibiotics or whatever. Carl gave me all I wanted to know about his visits with our 'Matariki man' here and after that it was just a case of getting the charge sheet all correctly typed up, by Terry's mate, the Crown Prosecutor."

Terry interjected, "He's no mate of mine!"

The Boss never missed a beat, replying with "That's funny, because he said the same thing about you. Listen, Terry, I have a plea deal to put forward. It's agreed by the Crown Prosecutor but there is a catch. Because he knows you, he will only act if you take his plea deal. If you fancy your chances in Court, he declines to act and will get someone from out of town to handle your case. That seems fair enough.

Anyways, here's the deal. You cop a guilty plea, and he will go for three years only. He reckons you could be inside for five years if you don't want his deal. There is a rider. He is an admirer of how the marae's handle their kids so it would have to be a clean deal. You take the guilty plea, and he will not chase anyone down on the maraes for being an accessory. What do you think?"

Terry, being cunning, would only add that he would think about it. But today's events had thrown him, and he would need a day or two to clear his mind. He did say that it would be a considerable nuisance for him to spend a night in jail and as he would obviously get bail. Was it really necessary to have him incarcerated for the evening. The Boss replied that he was only acting on the CP's instructions, so his hands were tied.

With that, the Boss was all wrapped up. I congratulated the Boss on his hunches and his follow up. All the while Terry was going on about our mutual admiration society and he would prefer it if the Boss just got on with it.

I was still a little in shock at how the Boss had handled the whole thing with Terry Hohepa and, to be honest, I was itching to get out and tell the Sarge what had happened.

The Boss took Terry out and over the road to our holding cells while I may have mentioned the situation to the Sarge. Over the road the lads were somewhat excited to have what amounted to a celebrity in their cells. With it being a Thursday evening, the cells were not that crowded, and Terry's only companion was a drunk and disorderly guy who kept Terry up for half the night with his singing.

On the next day Terry of course got his bail but the judge did warn him that he would be, if found guilty, probably facing a custodial term.

And that is how we found out about the 'Panel' operating in our fair city and of course we also found out about Terry and his operations.

In real life I always get annoyed when the story ends, and you don't know how much time they served. So, I'll make sure I put that right here.

Carl got his 16 years of jail time, well with four murders, a string of assaults and the sexual assault it was inevitable. Still. I hear he is behaving himself, and on his behaviour so far, he should be up for his parole.

Jeff Whitely and Craig Mansell both got their plea deal accepted by the Courts. They should be out in perhaps five and a half years' time with good behaviour.

Johnny Warburton got himself a brilliant lawyer. While throwing himself on the mercy of the Court, the lawyer also got a few points in about how Johnny Warburton was essentially a pawn in the grander scheme of things. Johnny ended up with just one year inside. He was out inside eight months.

I don't particularly think that an application to rejoin the Rotary Club would be met with much sympathy.

Terry Hohepa was a different case. Despite all of the people who came forward, or were coerced into coming forward, Terry did get jail time. He should have accepted the Crown Prosecutors deal. Terry got four years total to run consecutively. The compounding factor was the fact that he kept part of the proceeds of his crime. He will be out in about three and a half years' time. He also got disbarred from the Auckland Lawyers' register so he could never practise law again without a whole heap of jumping through hoops.

And last but by no means least, the Sarge beat me in the annual physical tests. He beat me by 11 seconds which was a bugger but at least we both passed.

And that is about it. As for me I'm quite happy being a Detective Sergeant here in Rotorua. I still visit my 'confidential informants' on a semi regular basis and I still live on my own in Holland Street.

Life is not that bad.

<u>Epilogue.</u>

It was a Wednesday evening.

Dave 'Ticker' Smith and Colin Woods were having their monthly meeting. Dave served his mate Colin a glass of Glenfiddich as they settled down to their business. Dave's wife had gone out to her weekly session of Line Dancing so they could talk openly about their business.

Dave's burning question was this," Why the hell did you mark that Tapsell lad down for a fatal. As far as I can see nearly everyone had him down for a good hiding."

Colin replied, "When his brief got him off, the little sod walked past me, and he smirked! The smarmy bastard knew he'd got off with it. I put a lot of work into that case and his dodgy brief got him off. He deserved it."

Dave Smith retorted, "Yes, well look at the mess it got us into. Half of the 'Panel', near enough, will end up doing time."

"Don't worry about it. There's still you, me, and Eric T. Add to that Dave Rosthern and we're nearly right enough for another 'Panel'. We'd better leave the Rotary lads alone for a month or two. Why don't you have a word with Dave and see if he can get a few of his Lodge mates involved. I've still got to get another fixer and it's probably best if we lay low for a month or two. You know, it still tees me off that Terry Hohepa used my fixer to do his dirty work. Still, he will get what he deserves."

Dave after a few moments thought, replied, "Moving on. I still reckon we should sound out Mark Hallam and see if he wants in."

Colin replied, "I reckon Mark is a bit of a do gooder. I think we'd be wrong to get him involved."

"So, get rid of him. Get him transferred. He liked his time in Napier".

Colin replied, "No way. He's a smartie. If I can keep an eye on him, I can still find out what he's up to and steer him away from looking too deep into the 'Panel'. No, I'd prefer to keep him under my wing until he's got past this thing."

Dave replied, reading from his list, "Next item our sale of drugs revenue is down over twenty-two hundred from last month. I know we had to get the Squad cars involved but it's still a substantial downturn. Have you had any feedback from the Black Power lads?"

Colin was ever ready to help, "Nothing from the Black Power lads. As long as they get regular supplies, they're happy. About our downturn. What do you reckon? Get me to bang a few heads together?"

Dave was quick to dismiss this, "God, no! When you bang heads together people get hurt. Let me have a word with them first. Oh, and if you're talking to Ronnie at the Mob, please tell him not to mention putting Mark on commission for Ronnie's better drug sales. That's going to do us no good. I still reckon it was a joke, but just have a word with him, next time you see him."

Colin replied, 'Leave that with me. Have you heard that this new Mayor is trying to make it tougher for out of town homeless to set up here."

Dave was a little more philosophical, "Another newbie into the job. Give him a month or two and he'll see he needs a few friends to get anything done on this council."

And that is where we will leave this story.

Police series

A series about crime in 'Rotorua'

Book 1 <u>The Panel</u>

It seems there is a 'panel' of people in Rotorua who decides if the local court system is giving a fair shake to the local criminals. If they get off lightly there may be further retribution available.

Book 2 <u>The Party</u>

A party takes place out in Hamurana area and the next day there is a murder case at the same address. Coincidence? Or is there more than meets the eye?

Book 3 <u>The Judge</u>

We appear to have a moral guardian at work. Then there is also another guy committing the same crime. Coincidence or not?

Book 4 <u>The War</u>

It's finally happened, and a gang war breaks out. The last thing the Police need is for someone else to get involved. And the last thing the Police need is always exactly what happens!

Book 5 <u>The payoff.</u>

It's a time when people need to decide who is on their side. And who can be let go? It's time for all friendships to be tested!

<u>Other work by the same Author</u>

Soul Purpose

Vol 1 & 11 & 111

A fiction work with something of a twist

He has returned.

The subtitle is "and it's so not what you think" Probably one of the most fun books I have written and probably the most amusing. The Son of God has returned, and he finds the world is in something of a state. Partly because of what he said and did a couple of thousand years ago on his last visit here. Yeah, it's all a bit confused now he is back. Let's see how he deals with it!

Mickey Carter: An angel with L-plates

It's funny and set in South Manchester. It's easy being an angel. Isn't it?

I have Angels at my table.

An interesting story set in England as natural disasters occur and somehow the higher levels of heaven are involved.

Danny Casanova's legacy

A fun story centred around a young guys first venture into the world of grown ups and doing what grown ups do. Or at least trying to!

Time and time again.

A book about past life experiences. Interestingly it only deals with past lives on planet earth.

About the Author

Andy has been writing for the last twenty years and has written a number of books over a wide variety of genre. His first book Sold over 5000 copies and he continues to write on whatever the mood takes him. Currently he is finishing Books on the crime scene in Rotorua, New Zealand. As always his books are not meant to be taken seriously. If you haven't laughed today, read one of Andy's books!